The Gnoll Credo

—

J. Stanton

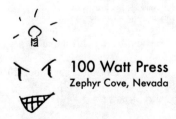

100 Watt Press
Zephyr Cove, Nevada

Author's website, including news, updates,
discussion forums, and more about the book:
www.gnolls.org

100 Watt Press
P.O. Box 10897
Zephyr Cove, NV 89448
www.100wattpress.com

Author photograph by Jeff Glass.
Front cover photograph by Colin Jackson,
modified under a Creative Commons attribution license.

Printed on acid-free, archival quality paper.

Library of Congress Control Number: 2010902978

ISBN 978-0-9826671-3-2

We all know this. Written for humans.

1. *We are born and we die. No one cares, no one remembers, and it doesn't matter. This is why we laugh.*
2. *Our pack, our children, our territory, the hunt, the kill, the battle. Health, full stomach, sharp weapons, your packmates next to you under the stars, seeing your child kill her first prey. These are important.*
3. *Anything else is needless complication, no matter how much fun it is.*
4. *If you can't eat it, wear it, wield it, or carry it, leave it behind.*

5. *Plan before hunting, discuss after hunting, hunt while hunting.*
6. *Lead, follow, or hunt alone. Success—first meat of kill, greater trust. Failure—less trust. Disaster—survivors eat you.*
7. *Expect trust outside the pack to be betrayed.*

8. *Two are much stronger than one. Three are much stronger than two. Ten are barely stronger than nine. Fifty are much stronger than ten, but barely stronger than forty.*
9. *An archer, a swordsman, and a scout are stronger than three swordsmen.*

10. *Stay alive. Hopeless battles are hopeless. Dead is dead.*
11. *Stay alive. Once you decide to kill, use all your skill, strength, and deception. Nobly dead is dead.*
12. *Die biting the throat.*

Education

———

"Human grows too slowly. Still suckling, can barely walk. Useless! I will be haouka before he can hunt for himself. Carry everywhere, back hurts."

"Yes, much too slowly. We still must learn more about humans, though."

"May I eat him? Fed on milk, sweet, tender." The gnoll grinned.

"Tender, yes, but full stomach only lasts two days, maybe three. You carried and suckled him for months. Wait another day, talk with packmates. Maybe one has a better idea."

And, as it turned out, someone did.

———

Both Jacob and Eleanor had been schoolteachers. They took turns running their inn and attached one-room schoolhouse, in which they educated anyone in the string of little villages between Odene and the frontier who needed or wanted to read and write. It was a small room, and even then, infrequently full.

Since they were on the trade route, though, there were always just enough caravans to support a steady trickle of children and apprentices needing to learn to add and subtract columns of figures—and, more profitably, stay in the common room at the inn until their caravan came back the other way. Then, there were local merchants and shopkeepers whose own children and apprentices needed the same skills. Finally, there were the few burghers who hoped to put on airs by exhibiting offspring who could speak like they were from Sostis and perhaps even quote dead politicians or philosophers, even if neither had any idea what they meant.

Between all of these, they managed a humble but comfortable living, finally selling the inn and retiring to a modest house in the northwestern woods, close enough to the local trade route to hear passing caravans, but perhaps an hour's ride from the nearest town. Life was slow, undemanding, and though one of their three children had recently been killed in a bandit raid, reasonably pleasant.

Then one dewy morning, while sitting on their porch watching the sun rise, they saw a war party of gnolls lope silently out of the trees.

They expected to die. Gnoll raids were relatively common this far north, and though they usually killed farmers and herdsmen, not retired schoolteachers, gnolls were never known to visit socially. With the calm that had allowed them to teach basic mathematics to generations of spoiled merchant brats, Jacob found Eleanor's hand, and squeezed it.

"I love you, dear heart."

"I love you, too."

Then everything changed.

Two of the gnolls stepped forward. One carried...a small human child? Naked, hair a mess, but reasonably clean and definitely alive—and awake now, making babbling, growling, yipping noises.

"Your child's child," said the other.

And there, in the arms of the monsters few expected to meet and live, was a healthy toddler with dark, curly hair, who really did look a lot like the baby they had last seen seven months ago—not long before news of the daring bandit raid that took their daughter's life, and her husband's, and those of the rest of the trading caravan.

"Joshua?" Eleanor stood. "Joshua?" She held out her arms, and the gnoll handed the toddler that might have been Joshua to her. "Is that really you, Josh?" She looked at the gnoll questioningly, eyes growing wet.

"Didn't know name," said the gnoll who had previously spoken.

Jacob stood too, in wonderment. "Well, he's got the hair, and—yes, the eyes too. Maybe miracles do happen, sometimes."

Eleanor handed Joshua to Jacob, and before she really thought about what she was doing, stepped forward and hugged the nearly naked, brutally fanged, wickedly clawed hyena-woman that towered over her, burying her face in the furry, bony chest. "Thank you. I don't understand, not at all, but thank you." She looked up, through a haze of tears, and the gnoll was looking down at her with what she swore was compassion, though she knew no one, including Jacob, would believe her.

There was a scrabbling noise, as of claws trying and failing to find purchase, on their wooden porch.

"Is Gryka. Feed her meat, not too much. You have books." It wasn't a question.

"Um, er, yes, what?" And the source of the scrabbling noise looked up at them with an unbearably cute but disturbingly toothsome grin.

"You keep six moons, maybe. Gryka dies, you die."

Jacob and Eleanor were overjoyed to see and hold their grandchild, whom they had thought lost in a bandit raid months ago; still terrified of the giant, rangy, savage animal-men who had just presented him to them, completely without introduction; and it slowly dawned on both of them that they had no idea whatsoever what they were going to do with the small, furry tornado of youthful energy that was already scent-marking the rough-hewn timbers of their tiny house.

The gnolls muttered and yipped briefly to Gryka[1], one by one.

And as quickly as they had arrived, they were gone.

Fearing the consequences should Gryka come to harm, yet finding her destructive capability to be considerable, Jacob and Eleanor found on that very first night that her appetite for bedtime stories far exceeded that of their own grandchild, who dozed off almost immediately. Gryka, however, stayed awake and brightly attentive all the way through, until Eleanor said "The End" and closed the cover, at which point she immediately laid down on the bed and curled herself

---

1: Pronounced "Gricka."

around Joshua, drawing a shout of alarm from Jacob.

"Get away from our child!" Jacob snapped, reaching for her. "Ow!"

Gryka growled and slapped at his arm, claws drawing tiny beads of blood.

"She's just cold, Jacob. Besides, we have no clothes or blankets for Joshua yet. And he doesn't seem to be complaining." It was true: Joshua was fast asleep.

"I am not sleeping in a bed with THAT," Jacob said flatly, pointing.

"I'm not sure we have a choice, dear," replied Eleanor.

And indeed, the bed was crowded that night.

Life suddenly became a lot noisier and more complicated. There were clothes and blankets to sew, sharp tools to hide, a bigger bed to build, two very hungry mouths to feed, and their shelves of books were one of their few possessions not to fall victim to claws and teeth that seemed to grow longer and sharper by the day. In fact, they soon found that any printed matter at all would do, at any time of day. "Read," Gryka demanded in her rough but intelligible grumble, pulling on an arm, and she would scuttle behind Jacob or Eleanor's chair, peering over their shoulder and intently tracking their finger as it wandered back and forth and down the page, following the path of the words they spoke.

"Are we teaching you to read, Gryka?" Jacob would ask with cocked eyebrow, disbelieving like everyone else that a savage gnoll could possibly understand or care about the written word. Gryka wouldn't reply to this, or to any other direct question, with anything more than the quizzical look a dog gives its master when it hasn't yet decided whether to obey—but if he or Eleanor paused too long in their reading, she would grab their hand and replace their finger on the page. Given her sharp claws and infrequent but destructive tantrums, both learned it was wise to comply. Besides, now that they were responsible for Joshua, both Jacob and Eleanor were terrified of what would happen if the gnolls returned and found Gryka gone.

Fortunately, Gryka spent much of her time outside, and though she often returned dirty or bloody, they quickly trained her to clean off her hands and paws before entering the house, a necessity she accepted without complaint. And though she preferred to visit the stream to do so, instead of carrying water back to the house in a bucket, she bathed herself as often as they did. However, they were never successful in teaching her to do anything with meat but wolf it down as quickly as possible, let alone use utensils, and soon simply gave it to her to eat outside. They found a benefit to this, though: instead of paying good money for cuts of meat, once Jacob realized he could justify buying anything at all by saying he and Eleanor had a new dog, he could simply take whatever bones, offal, or spoilage the butcher offered cheaply.

"Must be a big dog," said the butcher.

"Yes," Jacob replied.

"Good. Never know what's out there in the woods."

You have no idea, Jacob thought.

Several months passed in this way, and Gryka grew perceptibly taller in that short time—even faster than Joshua, who was growing quickly himself. The tiny house was full of stories read out loud, Joshua's happy toddler chatter, and the occasional tantrum, and though they certainly got less sleep than before, Jacob and Eleanor were happier than they had been in some time. Gryka seemed to be able to take care of herself, often disappearing entirely for much of the day, and their fear of her pack returning to find her gone had slowly been replaced by routine.

Gryka had begun to take down and page through some of the children's picture books. "How cute," Jacob said. "I guess she likes the pictures."

"I think she's reading, Jacob. Or trying, anyway. She's watched us read that one enough times."

"Nonsense. She always picks the books with animal pictures."

"Which word 'tortoise,' which word 'hare?'" Gryka asked, pointing to the page.

Eleanor gave Jacob a meaningful look as she bent to help Gryka. "Tortoise, there. Hare, there."

"Good story," Gryka said, closing the book, "but no hyenas."

Jacob burst into laughter. "Well, then."

From that day on, Gryka was full of questions, and since Joshua was just starting to speak in sentences, both Jacob and Eleanor had plenty of time to teach their strange but eager pupil. She seemed almost completely focused on vocabulary, and the few times Jacob or Eleanor asked her about what life with gnolls was like, she would simply shrug. "Play with others, learn to hunt."

One morning not long afterward, to their great surprise, Gryka came to them and said, very simply, "Head full now. Thank you for reading, explaining. I go." She hugged both of them, loped off into the woods, and that was that.

After a long, long pause, during which neither could find anything to say, Jacob threw back his head, laughed...and kept laughing.

"What's so funny, Jacob? I'm sad," Eleanor said. "I'll miss her, and we barely even got to say goodbye."

Jacob finally chuckled to a stop. "I'm sad, too, but we both knew it would probably happen like this. Besides, now we both know something extraordinary, something that I bet no one else knows...not even the big names at the University." He paused, thinking. "I wonder why literacy is suddenly important to the gnolls, and I wonder how long it'll take before anyone at the University, or anywhere else, even admits of the possibility?"

Eleanor smiled, eyes wet. "You're right. Let's never tell anyone; it's funnier that way, and no one will believe us anyway. I'll still miss her, though."

"So will I, dear heart. So will I."

Only later did Eleanor find a large blackened stone some distance from the house, the forest floor surrounding it littered with charred sticks that Gryka had been using to practice her writing, and only later did Jacob connect her departure with a missing pocket dictionary. And though they lived just long enough to raise their grandson Joshua, who eventually grew into a tall, handsome, and reasonably smart young man, neither saw Gryka or her pack again.

Departure

—

"Study *gnolls?*" the Duke snorted. "Why not just drink hemlock? Jump off the Black Cliffs?"

"I keep hearing stories from the merchant caravans," I replied. "At least the ones whose route goes all the way to the northwest frontier, past the desert."

"The ones that come back with all the exotic animal hides."

I nodded. "They say that's where they get them."

"From *gnolls?*" He snorted again.

"No, from the local tannery. But the merchants say the tannery gets most of them from gnolls, at least lately."

I shrugged. "Some even claim they'll see a gnoll in town, sometimes, and it isn't eating anyone and no one is running away."

"They're just bullshitting you," he growled. "That's the merchant's third favorite pastime, after cheating and short-changing."

"Could be," I said, "but I hear the same stories from differ-ent caravans. Usually the bullshit is different, too."

That got me his "I'm thinking" scowl. "If that's true, the gnolls are trading for something. But what? They don't build houses, don't wear trinkets, and the only thing I've ever known gnolls to want is us, dead." His scowl deepened. "They're good at it, too. Knights either find nothing or don't come back. Like fighting shadows. Glad I don't have any here, in my duchy."

"That's why I think they're worth studying. They use human weapons, we know that, and anything that good at guerilla tactics absolutely has to be intelligent. I don't buy the Church's line that they're just hyenas on their hind legs."

"They're scared!" he roared, laughing. "If gnolls were intel-ligent, they might have souls, and then the Church would have to send missionaries to save them!"

I didn't have to fake my laughter this time. "Makes trying to convert those Osengo nomads seem like cutting butter."

The Duke nodded. "That's why I keep you scholars around, running the University. You keep them busy chasing distant heathens, or just chasing your arguments, instead of making trouble for me. When they don't have anything to do, they start complaining that they need greater tribute for a bigger cathedral and more expensive junk to fill it up, or they start smelling heresy everywhere and pissing off my allies."

"Scholars love to argue, especially with ecclesiasticals." I grinned. "Please don't get assassinated, or we'll all have to leave Sostis before they arrest us for heresy."

"You knew the risk when you aligned with me instead of the bishopric," he shrugged. "You won't have any exceptional expenses on this trip, will you?"

"Only to the extent that it's farther than I usually travel for research," I said. "Getting to Odene is no problem, but after that I'll have to bribe my way across the Ghamor Desert, then pay off a few riverboat captains and probably at least one mountain guide."

"Can't you just follow the trade route around all that?" His eyes narrowed.

"The caravans take two months to go one way because they stop everywhere to trade, and if I follow the route without being part of one..." I let the consequence hang.

"Killed by bandits, second day out."

I nodded. "Other than that, just the usual supplies, and a big stash of tobacco."

"Didn't think you smoked." He arched an eyebrow.

"I don't," I grinned, "but once you get out of civilization, it's often better than money."

He laughed. "You've got common sense in that pointy head. If you had a trace of discipline I'd have made you a field officer, and if you had a trace of guile I'd have made you a diplomat. Does it have to be good tobacco?"

"No, but it has to smoke properly. Well-cured, not dry or moldy."

"Done. I support the University because it's cheaper than supporting the Church. Never forget that." Suddenly the Duke fixed me with an intense stare: as a military commander, he specialized in withering looks. "You're not deserting me, are you?"

I shook my head. "No, Captau."

"You're not committing an elaborate suicide, are you?"

"No, Captau."

"Good. Don't die, don't change your mind, and be back in four months. I've got a few counts- and barons-to-be coming this fall. Maybe even a mini-marquis, if the Keszcny alliance doesn't fall apart."

I nodded: despite what the Duke had said earlier, our main function was to keep the scions of nobility out of trouble—and out of the bishopric. "Yes, Captau."

"Dismissed." He waved his hand; I bowed and departed.

———

Travel is cheap, I thought: it's only expensive to travel safely. I'd be taking more silver with me than I liked, but a substantial part of it would be spent on the trip out, and no one expects scholars to have much money anyway.

Plus, I don't fit the stereotype of the timid, bespectacled academic. None of us do, because it takes strong physical presence, as well as a quick mind, to keep lordlings in line—being commoners, we can't actually order them to do anything—and it takes some weapon skills to return safely from pubs and theaters late at night, somewhat drunk, as is our habit. Though my distant Goidelic ancestry hasn't left me anything but an utterly incongruous name ("Aidan O'Rourke"), and my light brown hair is both grayer and thinner than it once was, I retain the vaguely ursine build of my father, my mother's long Northerner face, and the physical endurance of one who is too bored to stay on campus but too poor to own or keep a horse.

It'll be a long, uncomfortable journey, I thought, as I walked back to my modest room: better pack up and leave before I get waylaid by interdepartmental politics.

The Annotated Gnoll Credo

Aidan O'Rourke, Ph.D
Chairman, Department of Ethnology
Ten Bridges University, Sostis

Overview of the Gnoll Species (Homo crocuta)

Since gnolls are little-studied in our field (usually because their culture is thought, like most other feral animal-men, to be simplistic and uninteresting) and there are many misconceptions about them, I will first present an overview of the gnoll species, with some basic facts.

Gnolls are tall, bipedal humanoid hyenas.

Though hyenas are a social species with strong pack structure, they are much more closely related to the civet and mongoose than to the wolves they superficially resemble.[1] There are three extant species of hyena; the spotted hyena is largest, most powerful, and most common, and modern gnolls are clearly related in appearance and social structure to the spotted hyena. (Gnolls more closely resembling striped or brown hyenas have been rumored for many years, but no reliable sightings or evidence have been confirmed.)

Gnoll legs are digitigrade, with larger but hyena-like rear paws tipped with non-retractable claws. Their torso and arms are similar to a human's (though longer and bonier due to their height), with somewhat knobby elbow joints and slightly "loose" shoulders, which seem to take impacts and falls without dislocating or separating as easily as a human's. Their human-like hands, in contrast, are thick and blocky to support the short, powerful, semi-retractable claws that tip

---

1: Thus, the best answer to the common question "Are hyenas dogs or cats?" is "Neither. They're hyenas."

each finger and thumb, and the muscles that support their tenacious grip make their forearms as large as their upper arms.

In contrast to their generally lean, wiry build, gnolls have a thick, powerful neck, curved forward to support a scaled-up spotted hyena's head and ears. Their body is covered with coarse yellowish fur, reversed to form a short mohawk-like mane atop the neck and head, that grows more or less shaggy according to climate and season—though gnolls seem to prefer warm or hot weather, and are not known to permanently inhabit any region that receives snow. (Summer and winter migrations are uncommon, but do occur in some mountainous areas.) Their pelt is typically spotted on the back, arms, and legs, and their muzzles, hands, and paws, as well as the tip of their tail, are always black. It is said that the spots slowly fade with age.

A typical adult gnoll stands 7-8 feet tall if she stands fully erect—which, like most bipedal digitigrade species, she rarely does except when asserting dominance. Usual relaxed standing height is between 6½ and 7½ feet, and gnolls generally weigh between 210-260 pounds.[2] Much of their mass is concentrated in the neck musculature, which accounts for their nearly emaciated build, and inspired the famous observation, "I guess if I were that skinny I'd eat anything, too."

Gnolls easily outrun humans, but cannot run nearly as fast as wolfmen, lion-men, or other bipedal digitigrades, who have longer and more powerful legs for their size. As such, they are not ambush hunters. The gnolls' success lies in their endurance; they can maintain their steady, loping gait for hours at a time, running their prey to exhaustion if it's too fast

---

2: Females are taller and heavier than males: they tend towards the high end of these ranges, while males tend towards the low end.

to catch immediately.[3] Typically, a gnoll hunting party will find a prey herd, identify the weakest members, then attack to scatter the herd and single one out. One gnoll is chosen as the tracker, whose responsibility is to lead the pack to the chosen prey as it flees; the rest simultaneously follow the tracker and prevent the prey from rejoining the herd. Once the tracker judges that the prey is sufficiently tired and weak to kill safely, and assuming she has not lost its trail, the rest of the gnolls converge, bring it down, and eat it.

Though gnolls usually stay in their territories, they can easily cover 70-80 linear miles in a day over open ground. Voyages of over 120 miles/day are known, and given typical speeds used when tracking prey, 200 miles/day would be achievable, though not verified.[4]

The most common misconception about gnolls, like spotted hyenas, is that they are primarily scavengers of the dead and others' kills. In reality, both are primary predators, and despite their reputations, extensive field observation has shown that lions actually steal hyena kills more often than hyenas steal a lion kill. Thus, the spotted hyena's popular reputation as a sneaky scavenger of the noble lions is much less realistic than the picture of studious, hard-working hyenas frequently having their daily wages stolen by the bigger, more powerful, and lazier lions. The theft is not all one-sided, though; hyenas sometimes get their own back

---

3: Spotted hyenas are also endurance hunters: they can run at forty miles per hour for up to two miles, and have been observed pursuing prey for over ten miles. In order to support such long hunts, a hyena's heart is twice the size of a lion's, despite a body only one-half to one-fifth as large—so from a strictly scientific point of view, "hyena-hearted" is a greater compliment than "lion-hearted."

4: Gnolls prefer to hunt and travel at night, when it's cooler. Their night vision is excellent, and they have no fear of the dark, themselves being the monsters the rest of us fear to encounter.

through more intelligent pack tactics and sheer force of numbers. Short-lived but bloody wars between the two species have been known to break out.[5]

The antipathy between the two species extends to their humanoid analogs. The hatred of gnolls for lion-men, and vice versa, is nearly legendary, though as humanoids both are more evenly matched: leonids have greater speed, agility, and raw strength, but gnolls employ more sophisticated tactics and have no cultural imperative to prove bravery against bad odds. In places where both exist, territories do not overlap, and gnoll packs will defend against leonid incursions just as fiercely, if not more so, than those of other gnolls.

Gnolls, like spotted hyenas, are obligate carnivores. They eat anything that is meat, was once meat, contains meat, or has meat attached to it. Like hyenas, gnolls can crush and digest any bone that fits between their premolars, and they typically consume every part of their prey, leaving only a bloodstain and some trampled grass. Furthermore, they can digest carrion, without sickness or other ill effect, that other predators won't touch. In fact, the easiest way to think of both hyenas and gnolls is as a vehicle for directing meat into the most powerful jaws on land, with the digestive system to back it up.

5: Usually lions win these conflicts due to their much greater size, strength, and agility, especially if the much larger males are present: lions are two to five times the size of hyenas. However, groups of spotted hyenas have been known to kill healthy lionesses, and are the only four-legged predator known to do so.

Since the two species fill the same ecological niche and hunt much of the same prey, conflict between them is intense. They will obliterate each others' territorial scent markings, defend their territories against each other, and some of their behaviors are difficult to interpret as anything but hatred: lion males will kill hyenas even when no food is in dispute, and when hyenas do manage to kill a lion, they will frequently roll around on the carcass before tearing into it, as if gloating. Both species will also eat the others' cubs whenever they find them.

A Brief History of the Credo

As a leading ethnographer and ethnolinguist, I had heard rumors that the gnolls of the far northwest frontier actually engaged in limited commerce with humans—as opposed to the rest of Human civilization, which usually finds itself at war with gnolls any time it decides to build on new land instead of simply hunting in it or traveling through it. Finally, progress having ground to a halt on my Orcish-Human dictionary, I decided to undertake the weeks-long voyage, an account of which could fill an entire book by itself.

Upon arriving in a tiny village approximately at the end of nowhere, I promptly encountered Gryka—a seven-and-a-half-foot-tall humanoid hyena is difficult to miss in a hamlet of perhaps a hundred, even if she only shows up once every week or so. I was just starting to debate the wisdom of a plan that involved long solo contact with creatures that could eat my head in two bites—and were known to do so when provoked—when she spotted me across the village square, closing the distance between us in an alarmingly short time.

"Aidan O'Rourke. What do you want?" she boomed: her voice was rough and intimidatingly deep, but surprisingly intelligible. (I quickly learned that gnolls never use pleasant-ries, which I initially interpreted as a dominance tactic. Well, I was happy to submit to her dominance, considering she could probably use my head as a toothbrush.)

"I study other races and other languages. I want to learn about gnolls."

I fully expected her to laugh at me or be offended. Instead, she simply asked "What do you want to know?"

Given the length of my journey and the completely unex-pected (to an ethnologist) appearance of a straightforward reply, the words spilled out as if her question had pulled a cork in my brain. "I want to know if you have a religion or a philosophy, and if so, what it is. I want to learn your language. I want to learn everything I can about your culture. I want—"

She shushed me with a quick gesture. "Too much talking. Ask one question."

I thought for a moment. "Do gnolls have a written religion or philosophy of life?"

Gryka cocked her head for a long moment. "No, but I write it for you. Come back tomorrow, same time." And with that, she loped out of town to the west.

I stood there, mildly dumbfounded, and finally remembered to close my mouth. A couple villagers laughed at me. "Not much for small talk, is she?"

The questions rattled around my head like dice in a cup. How had she known my name and what I looked like? Did the gnolls have an undiscovered oral tradition? Could she actually read and write, or was I going to be the human victim of a macabre gnoll joke? Did gnolls even have a sense of humor? (They would occasionally laugh hysterically, like spotted hyenas, but no one really knew why. I've studied them for years, and now I have a definitive answer to my question: yes, they do, and I know why as much as any human can. I'll talk about that later.)

In other words, I was starting to feel the excitement of a thoroughly interesting ethnological problem.

I half expected Gryka to return with the bloody skull of a prey animal, or simply not show up at all—but as I sat outside the local general store watching the hot, dusty afternoon crawl by, she walked straight up to me and dropped a large, much-folded piece of paper in my lap.

I opened it and saw...a merchant's column of daily figures. "Turn it over."

She stood next to me, apparently waiting for me to read it. I turned it over, revealing a large block of closely, meticulously-written gibberish—in the Roman alphabet, but gibberish no less. "What language is this, Gryka?"

"Ours. I try your language, but words missing. You don't know ours?"

"No, I don't." No one did. Back in civilization, anyone who got close enough to gnolls to hear more than a few words was generally eaten.

She gave me the wide, toothy, slightly lopsided grin[6] I came to know so well. "Then come with me."

I spent most of my summer in that tiny, isolated village, grabbing like a drowning man at whatever knowledge Gryka dropped near me as I attempted to translate what I soon came to think of as "that damned page of gibberish." It was completely unlike any other field study I'd done: most involve a long, slow process of gaining the trust of a single group member, often through bribes; slowly learning their language and culture and taboos (which are like snares, or leg-hold traps...it's hard to find where they are without setting them off); then wheedling an introduction to the greater group so I can get to the real knowledge, guarded like treasure by the priest/shaman caste.

In contrast, Gryka didn't seem to place any particular value on her knowledge or that of the gnolls in general; her

---

6: Gnolls are very expressive once you know how to interpret their faces. Symmetry is a sign of seriousness—if a gnoll bares her teeth at you in a fully symmetrical snarl, you are most likely her lunch. If a gnoll bares her teeth at you but leaves one eye slightly more open than the other, or the grin is wider on one side (or, usually, both), this has a similar meaning to the human wink or raised eyebrow: it modifies the aggression with playfulness, as if saying, "Come on, this is going to be fun, and you might not actually die."

Keeping in mind, of course, that a gnoll's rough play can easily be fatal to humans.

only constraint seemed to be whether she had anything else to do at the time. If not, she would give me her full attention and earnestly (as far as I could tell) try to answer all of my questions. Some lucky days I'd get three hours with her, then a week would go by in which I wouldn't get twenty minutes. And on some rare, precious days, she would lead me out of town to speak with the rest of the pack; though neither Gryka nor any other gnoll ever mentioned it, I was clearly not welcome except by invitation, and unlike any of my projects before or since, I never tried to find them and make observations on my own.

My translation was complicated by the fact that gnolls had no written language: Gryka had simply written everything in what she considered to be our closest phonetic equivalent. To an untrained human ear, the gnolls' language sounds more like soft growls, yips, and grumbles,[7] and she was essentially making up a pronunciation guide as she went along. I was amazed that she could even tell what she had previously written! However, she was eager to improve her English skills and vocabulary, and translating her untitled document served both our purposes.

As the translation slowly took shape, my excitement grew. Not only was I probably the first human to understand what I quickly and uncreatively dubbed Gnollish, I realized that Gryka's document was much simpler and more powerful than the simplistic "big man" creation myths of most primitive tribes. Frankly, they're mostly of a piece: the first god blows a booger out of his nose, or waves his hands, or makes companions and they fight, or just gets bored—and there's the world

---

7: Gnolls can hear much better than humans can, and speak softly among themselves except when arguing or displaying strong emotions. In contrast, the loud, growling *whoop* with which they call or warn packmates can carry for miles in still air.

but it's still boring so he makes people too, and it's basically a bedtime story for children that doesn't really mean or explain anything.

In contrast, the Gnoll Credo isn't a myth at all. It's not even a legal code, with a fixed set of rules and punishments. It's simply a description of the world and how the gnolls survive in it, and it has a stark, desolate beauty that still makes me stop and think every time I look at it.

I shall someday tell the rest of the stories of my time with Gryka, but I believe this to be the most important. I have done my best to translate her original writing into English; when I gave my first complete draft to her and asked if it seemed right, she shrugged and said *"Kazhda."*[8] She would approve of my subsequent improvements, even giving me encouragement ("Much better now. Sounds more like gnolls, not humans") but the end result was always *"Kazhda."* I never quite understood whether she felt that English simply was not up to the task, or whether it was a more subtle concept, in which naming and constraining the truth instantly turned it into at least a partial lie. I suspect both.

In any case, here it is: the answer Gryka wrote to my question "Do gnolls have a written religion or philosophy of life?" I have tentatively titled it "The Gnoll Credo."

8: The word frequently translated as "Close enough" (*"Kazhda"*), like many Gnollish words, is a noun which can also be used as an adjective.

Kazhda is a strike that hits the enemy or prey animal and causes damage, but is not accurate or strong enough to kill by itself: an arrow through the shoulder that misses the heart, a bite that tears muscle but misses the artery, etc. A successful strike, but insufficient by itself and requiring more work to make the kill.

However, it also connotes something like "And what did you really expect under the circumstances?" An arrow shot too quickly from a bad position, a child trying to bring down her first prey, a male asking to mate with a female: a situation in which unqualified success is theoretically possible, but not to be expected.

Annotated Text of the Credo

In order to preserve the simple, direct nature of the Credo, I have had to cut corners with the translation. This is because many of its simple, fundamental Gnollish words cover broad conceptual ground that a single English word cannot encompass, or alternatively, have precise connotations that the closest English word does not share. I will explain some of these below. (I do not plead special circumstances, as this is a problem for translators of any language.)

First, and perhaps most importantly, the original document has no title or line numbers. "The Gnoll Credo" is just the name I've given it, and the short explanation at the top ("We all know this. Written for humans") is its true beginning.

> **1: *We are born and we die. No one cares, no one remembers, and it doesn't matter.[*] This is why we laugh.***

[*]: This sentence is actually a very short Gnollish phrase (*"Hazrah nachti"*) that can be translated trivially as the rhetorical question "Who cares?" Its meaning, however, is much deeper and more complex, also containing elements (besides those in my direct translation) of the English expressions "So it goes" and "No witness, no body, no crime," a cheerful fatalism[9] usually only seen in recklessly warlike species like

---

9: Fatalism is not precisely the correct term; gnolls apparently have no concept of fate or destiny, and indeed, Gryka found the concept strange. ("Future just in head," she said. "Always changing anyway.")

However, though they always do everything they can to survive and plan for the future, gnolls seem to cheerfully accept that they can neither predict nor control it.

the orc, and the strong implication that whoever asked the question should have already known this would be the answer.

Despite their strong pack instinct, gnolls celebrate the deeds of living individuals with gusto and brio, but they seem to quickly lose interest in remembering the deeds of the dead. They may dramatically modify their behavior as a result of the action or discovery of an individual gnoll (see my forthcoming monograph "The Dolhin Incident"), but apparently have no interest in venerating the original accomplishment. In all my time with gnolls, I never caught a single reference to the name of a gnoll who had died outside the living memory of those present—and even then, references to the dead occurred only in the context of stories involving the living.

> *2: Our pack, our children, our territory[**], the hunt, the kill, the battle. Health[*], full stomach, sharp weapons, your packmates next to you under the stars, seeing your child kill her[***] first prey. These are important.*

[*]: "Health" is a desperately poor cousin to the Gnollish word *nikai,* which means so much more than an absence of sickness. Unmodified, *nikai* is a clean killing bite or blow. As a modifier, it implies both correctness and optimality, though not necessarily perfection. It is in contrast to, though not opposite, the word *kazhda.*

In this context (i.e., applied to gnolls in general, or any individual gnoll), *nikai* means that one's mind and body are functioning optimally, implying purposeful training and fitness for the tasks of life, capable of striking that clean killing blow.

An aside: gnolls do not seem to draw the sharp line between mind and body that humans typically do. They generally regard thinking as just another bodily function, like breathing or digestion, and the brain is just more meat to them.

[**]: The word I have translated as "territory" (*"aregi"*) is only one of a family of related words, all describing types and characteristics of a pack's territory, and all with many connotations.

Aregi is ideal territory. It is undisputed by other gnolls; it is unspoiled by human industrial activity such as logging, mining, or cities; it doesn't contain too many humans or other competing climax predators; it contains clean year-round water sources; and it is sufficiently large and rich in prey to easily and sustainably feed the pack, even in lean years.

Many packs consider any human presence at all to break *aregi*, but Gryka's pack tolerates a few hunters and pack stations, and allows limited grazing so long as the shepherds pay a "tax" of a few animals every year to the pack. Gryka's ability to read and write, though minimally and crudely, made this arrangement enforceable (humans have a lamentable tendency to renege on spoken bargains), and I am convinced it is the sole reason that commerce between our races exists in the Northwest and nowhere else.

[***]: Unlike English, Gnollish has generic, non-sexual pronouns. I generally translate them as female, since gnoll packs are matriarchal.

Like spotted hyenas, gnoll females are visibly larger and more aggressive than the males, and the lowest-ranking female outranks the highest-ranking adult male. Even newborn cubs outrank males, and though (unlike hyenas) gnoll mothers often allow fathers to guard their own cubs while they hunt, females tend to view male packmates as a necessary evil, with an attitude somewhere between amusement and irritation.

I once asked Gryka if gnolls married or mated for life like humans do. "Like humans do sometimes," she corrected me, and settled into that quizzical expression that let me know she was seriously considering the question. "Sometimes, but only if children survive, are strong. If not, why mate with same male again?"

"Do the women choose the men, or do the men choose the women?" I asked.

"Females always choose." She grinned, and it's true: gnoll females control reproduction absolutely. I have since learned how and why, but that is a whole another paper in itself.

3: Anything else is needless complication[*], no matter how much fun it is.

[*]: The word *"nerga,"* which I translate as "needless complication," apparently originated as *"nerga-nerga-nerga,"* a crude imitation of human speech. It is derived from the human tendency (to gnolls, at least) to talk too much and too quickly, with meaning either esoteric, useless, or misleading to the relatively simple goals and mind of the gnoll. Any excessively complicated plan is generally dismissed as *nerga,* as is one excessively contingent on future actions of those outside the pack.

Most gnolls have weak aptitude for the fields generally considered to denote intelligence, but they have a good sense of their own limitations—and derive a great deal of amusement from seeing the complicated plans of humans go awry, as they often do. A well-timed *"nerga,"* said *sotto voce,* is often enough to send a pack of gnolls into hysterical laughter.

4: *If you can't eat it, wear it, wield it, or carry it, leave it behind.*

Gnolls are nomadic within their territory, and do not build houses. They sometimes build small shelters in frequently-used sleeping places to keep off the sun, the rain, and the worst of the wind, which they will use when in the area—but they have no particular attachment to them, and are just as happy to use a convenient cave or stand of trees. (Gnolls aren't known to inhabit any place that receives winter snow, or is otherwise cold enough to require protection beyond sleeping curled up with packmates.)

Though they will defend their territory with their lives, gnolls don't bother to possess anything which they can't physically carry with them at all times. Everything else is generally considered *nerga,* and they find the human tendency to accumulate possessions, especially decorative possessions with no obvious function, endlessly amusing. "Like magpies!" said Gryka, roaring with laughter. "Build huge nest, fill with shiny junk."

The single partial exception to this is weapons and armor, which gnolls will always use in battle if they can—particularly swords, which allow them to use their long reach to best advantage, and the longbow[10], which their height allows them to carry much more easily than a human. However, they do not carry their weapons and armor around continually, usually preferring to hunt using only their own extremely powerful claws and jaws.

10: Strictly speaking, the gnoll bows I have seen are lightly recurved flatbows, not traditional round-sectioned longbows—though they are tall enough to be considered longbows. (Gnolls have long arms even for their considerable height, and need a very long draw to match.)

I asked Gryka about this; she said "Carry weapons or armor, slows us down, makes noise. Harder to chase." She grinned a big, feral, symmetrical grin. "Also, more fun to run prey down, bite throat, taste hot blood."

Sure, I thought, shivering.

When I asked her where she kept the sword, bow, and armor I saw her wear occasionally, she just chuckled and said "Big territory."

5: Plan before hunting, discuss after hunting, hunt while hunting.

"Plan" and "discuss" are our closest equivalent to the Gnollish words for "plan/debate future action" and "reflect/debate past action," which cover one's own thoughts as well as discussing them with others. This is a wonderfully succinct summation of the need to plan ahead and learn from results, but also to stay totally focused on the task at hand while performing it.

6: Lead, follow, or hunt alone.[*] Success—first meat of kill, greater trust.[**] Failure—less trust. Disaster—survivors eat you.

[*]: This sentence strongly implies "...but don't complain," and I've heard it used as such. "Child wants to become adult, first lesson," Gryka said, laughing.

[**]: The English translation to 'trust' is accurate—but the word has far more import and impact in Gnollish, because it implies higher rank, authority, and responsibility in the pack. High-ranking females generally use their authority to eat first

at kills[11] and to reproduce more often, and they will generally choose to mate with high-ranking males.

Unlike hyenas, female rank is not purely hereditary. Exceptional deeds, or sustained good or bad judgment, can cause a shift—though in practice, rank is relatively stable, usually only changing when packmates reach adulthood or die.

I asked Gryka if her pack has ever eaten anyone as punishment for failure. "No, but we make neighbors eat their leader once," she said, with a big, toothy grin.

7: Expect trust outside the pack to be betrayed.

Just as with the previous line, "trust" involves both authority and responsibility. Since it requires a close, ongoing, mutually dependent relationship with packmates, gnolls generally hold no hope of extending trust to humans, or even to others outside their pack. If they appear to do so, it is generally because they believe the arrangement to be enforceable, or that its failure would be unimportant.

"Why I learn to read and write," Gryka says. "Humans say 'Why do you kill, eat George's[12] sheep?' We say 'Too many, we agreed thirty, no more.' George says 'No, you say forty,' every time." She snorted. "Always. Then fights, maybe kill George, patrols, king sends knight or two. Now, we show George, other humans paper with writing. 'Thirty sheep, no more,' and George's mark. Grumble some, but no fighting."

I smiled ruefully.

"Also, better for George. Big men come from city, say 'So much land! I bring hundreds of sheep now, hire mercenaries,

---

11: The Gnollish word for "alpha female" translates literally as "first-eater."
12: Gryka found the name "George" endlessly amusing for some reason, and used it to refer to any human whose name she didn't know—or had forgotten.

chase you off.' George laughs, says 'Better ask gnolls first.'
Now George is happy, saves fat sheep for us." She grinned.

> *8: Two are much stronger than one. Three are much stronger than two. Ten are barely stronger than nine. Fifty are much stronger than ten, but barely stronger than forty.*

This line serves two purposes. First, gnolls are pack hunters, and gain strength in numbers. Second, it shows that gnolls understand the law of diminishing returns, at least as it applies to numbers in hunting and combat. Because of this, gnolls generally hunt in small breakaway groups, and unless the hunt is for extremely large, dangerous game or is taking place in disputed territory, the entire pack is rarely involved.

Every gnoll I've questioned seems to be able to abstract these understandings to other fields—and remains almost completely disinterested in doing so except as it serves her immediate interests. For example: as far as I can tell, Gryka learned to read and write entirely so that her pack could enter into contracts with humans. Though she was perfectly capable of writing down concepts, and did so upon my request, she had never previously done so. I don't know if the idea simply never occurred to her, or whether it had but she dismissed it as irrelevant.

> *9: An archer, a swordsman,[**] and a scout[*] are stronger than three swordsmen.*

Gnoll packs also gain strength from division of labor. For hunting, trackers, harriers, killers; for battle, scouts, archers, swordsmen. These are not fixed roles; though individuals tend to assume one or the other based on their skill and experience, they will often rotate roles to train children or simply for a change of pace, especially on easy hunts, and the demands of a particular situation always take priority. "Prey bolts past you, you are tracker now," Gryka says.

[*]: The word "scout" also translates as "tracker," one whose role is to forge ahead searching for signs of prey or the enemy, or to lead the party to prey or an enemy already identified.

[**]: Again, Gnollish has generic, non-sexual pronouns, which I generally translate as female: I only use "swordsmen" in this instance because "swordswoman" is clumsy.

> *10: Stay alive. Hopeless fights are hopeless.*
> *Dead is dead.*
>
> *11: Stay alive. Once you decide to kill, use all*
> *your skill, strength, and deception. Nobly dead*
> *is dead.*
>
> *12: Die biting the throat.*

Gnolls do not have the concept of the "noble death" like orcs and some humans...they believe it is better to survive than to die while achieving revenge, and they will stay out of conflicts they honestly believe they have no chance of winning. They also have absolutely no sense of fairness in deadly combat. Once they decide to kill, all tactics are in play, including dirty tricks and outright cheating.[13] Furthermore,

---

13: I had a difficult time explaining the concept of "dueling" to Gryka. "Rules for fighting, we understand," she said. "Shouldn't kill, cripple packmate over food, for rank. Still don't understand dueling, though."

"Dueling is just rules for deadly combat. Same weapons for both, no cheating, no tricks. The only difference should be skill, so the best man wins."

"Rules for killing? *Kill other, don't die.*" She snorted. "Other deserves death, give them chance anyway? Stupid!" And I was never able to convince her otherwise.

any attack on what one might believe to be a single gnoll or a small group will almost always end with a fight against all packmates within earshot, especially within a pack's territory.

There are few fighters more vicious in the face of certain death: no matter the odds, a cornered, outnumbered, or injured gnoll will never, ever give up, and will often take an alarming number of attackers with her even when mortally wounded. Gnolls often survive impossible situations because their attackers are unwilling to take the casualties necessary to kill them.

A famous story from my hometown involves a skilled swordsman who cleanly beheaded an attacking gnoll. Unfortunately, the detached head struck the swordsman's arm as it fell, and the gnoll's powerful jaws caught and crushed the arm before the head expired, still firmly clamped to the ruined remains of the swordsman's arm—which had to be amputated above the elbow.

As a result of this relentless focus on survival, and of their low population compared to humans, gnolls never engage in formal battles—unlike orcs, who seem to relish the glory and discipline of the military. Gnolls always use guerilla tactics, including ambushes, assassinations, snares and booby traps, always avoid direct confrontation whenever possible, and their excellent night vision means they almost always attack in the dark. Add powerful, accurate longbows, superhuman speed and endurance, and a complete lack of infrastructure to burn or destroy, and it's easy to see how a pack of gnolls can defend their territory against a much larger army.

For this, the gnolls are derided as cowardly, but their effectiveness is undeniable. Troop detachments sent to rid an area of gnolls usually arrive to find no gnolls at all—and their perimeter guards and horses dying in alarming numbers each night. The gnolls have also noticed that a mounted knight isn't particularly effective without his mount, and while it's against all codes of chivalry to shoot or hamstring a horse, this does not bother them in the least.

In relation to the twelfth and last line of the Credo ("Die biting the throat"), it is worth noting here the life cycle of the gnoll, because it and their attitude towards death account for much of the human race's strained relationship with gnolls.

Gnolls mature very quickly, reaching sexual maturity at six and full size at eight. Adult gnolls maintain their strength (and, apparently, their sexual potency) until old age begins at approximately 30 years, at which point they deteriorate rapidly, dying within a year or two.

However, in reality, it is unheard of for a gnoll to die of old age.

Gnolls know when their body begins to break down: the word "*haouka*" translates almost perfectly as "time of self-betrayal," and is used as both noun and adjective, describing both the time and one who has entered it. In keeping with their credo of "Die biting the throat," a gnoll in *haouka* will take progressively greater risks, performing more and more daring feats of reckless bravery until she is killed. It is not unknown for *haouka* from different packs to join forces and attack humans, especially in places where territories are clearly established and relatively stable.

This is why all the Earth races suffer continual raiding parties of gnolls: it is how dying gnolls commit ritual suicide. *Haouka,* the ongoing sacrifice of the aged, is the primary way in which a pack maintains and expands its territory, battling other gnolls, humans, and anything else. Only a serious conflict will involve younger gnolls as attackers.

Some packs have started a tradition in which *haouka* scarify themselves to mark the beginning of their "time of self-betrayal." Usually this begins with a simple X on the shoulders or the face around the eyes, but as the nervous system deteriorates, a gnoll will mutilate herself repeatedly because, as Gryka says, "The pain helps her concentrate."

This outward sign allows other gnolls to give a wide berth and lots of tolerance to a pack member who is searching for an excuse to fight to the death. Furthermore, it means that our previous idea that the mysterious "Scarred Clan" of gnolls is primarily responsible for attacks on civilization is false, and continuing attempts to wipe out that "clan" will remain fruitless.

A Final Note

I have read the original Gnollish document to other gnolls, making clear that it was written by another gnoll, not by me—and after breaking into hysterical laughter multiple times during my reading, they all say the same thing: *"Kazhda."*

I finally asked one pack what could be done to improve it. After a long silence, the highest-ranking male spoke. *"Not to say it at all. We know it already. Hearing words just confuses us."*

"But how do you teach your children to live?" I asked, in my halting Gnollish. *"How do you remember what is important and what is nerga?"*

He waved one clawed hand at the darkness around the fire. *"The world tells us that every day."*

From: Aidan O'Rourke, Chairman, Department of Ethnology
To: All instructors
Subject: Gnollish Pronunciation

The relentless butchering of Gnollish pronunciation around here forces me to write a quick guide to the basics. Read this, initial it, return it to me, I'll post it in the refectory once everyone's seen it, and I'll take it down once the carnage ceases.

Gnollish plosives are slightly softened—"k" towards "gh", "t" towards "d"—unless explicitly hardened by a leading "t". Example: "Tkaidah!", an expression of surprise. The "t" is silent but creates a very hard "k".

Syllabic stresses are very light. If in doubt, pronounce with equal emphasis.

haouka: hah-OO-kah. Three syllables...NOT "how-kah."
hazrah nachti: hahz-RAH nahx-TEE. The "ach" is alveolar, as in "Achtung," because of the following "t".
kazhda: KAHZH-dah.
nikai: NEE-kye. The "ee" sound is shortened and brought forward somewhat, towards "ih".
aregi: ar-EGG-ee. The leading "a" is nearly schwa.
nerga: NER-gah.

Gryka: GRIH-kah. All female names end in a nearly-schwa "a".
Chuka: CHOO-kah. "Ch" is pronounced normally due to the vowel following it.
Nako: NAH-koh. All male names end in "o", or occasionally "u". The "oh" sound is closed slightly, towards "oo".
Toku: TOH-koo. The "oo" sound is opened somewhat when

used at the end of male names, towards "oh", and the two are difficult to distinguish. I believe this to be just a difference in local dialect.

<u>Nyko</u>: NIH-koh.

<u>Roko</u>: ROH-koh.

<u>Taeku</u>: TAY-koo. The "ay" sound is closed slightly, towards "eh".

Pronouncing these words like a gnoll is beyond the scope of a single page—but this guide will at least get you understood.

Laughter

——

As we did so often that first summer, Gryka and I were sitting on a rock on a small rise overlooking the scrubby grasslands that stretched for miles out of town to the north, discussing Gnollish words and concepts and how to express them in English, while I scribbled notes that I would only partially decipher back at the inn that night.

Well, I was sitting, anyway. She would shift position every minute or two, watching me as we talked, but always from a different place, and often I would have to stand up to talk to her because she was behind me. "You make me dizzy," I said. "Can't you just sit or stand still?"

"Here alone," she said simply. "Must keep watch."

I was here, I almost said, but I knew I didn't count, for either hunting or defense. "Who's going to attack you here? You're smack in the middle of your territory."

"*Haouka* from other pack, maybe. Sneak in, make kill. Also, might see lunch." She grinned.

And that's her reality, right there, I thought. No wonder the Credo is what it is.

"I feel sad for you," Gryka said to me, out of the blue.

"Why?"

She stared at me intently. "You are mated to your learning —but learning cannot hunt with you. Learning cannot sleep with you when it's cold. Learning cannot bear your children. And the rest of your pack does not share or celebrate your successes, it envies them. Yes?"

Sometimes the truth is so perfect that it leaves you speech-less, simply because there is nothing to be added or subtracted, nothing to do but admire its terrible beauty even as it rips out your still-beating heart and sterilizes the bleed-ing cavity.

This I did, for a time that could have been seconds and could have been minutes. This feral creature, barely literate and half-human at the best of times, had laid bare my entire existence as casually and completely as her fearsome jaws snapped the neck of a fleeing antelope.

I saw leaves rustle gently in the wind. I saw a mongoose poke its head out from behind a small rock. And from some-where within the vast, frozen vacuum that had so recently been my soul, the beginnings of laughter twisted my lips and snorted air out my nose.

Gryka was still staring at me intently, impassively.

It got worse. I saw a flock of weaverbirds high overhead

and heard warthogs rooting in the bushes to my right. I was grinning widely now and bouncing with each ridiculous convulsion. Stupid! Stupid! Stupid!

I whooped hysterically. The sound was terrifyingly inhuman, and it startled me. Who knew I could even make a sound like that?

Who am I, anyway? I knew that I used to have an answer to that question, but no answers remained in the cold black vacuum. Ridiculous! I whooped again, and the sound was comforting this time. I am that which can make this terrifying noise, that's what, and even that doesn't matter, and fuck you. Whoo! Ha!

Gryka was grinning so widely now that she looked like her head was going to split open. The thought was so preposterous that I lost it completely.

Apparently, so did she, because the howling doubled in volume and intensity. Tears streamed down my face as I sobbed and whooped. I no longer knew what came from my throat and what from hers. I heard water running underground. I knew the focus of a hawk as it stooped on an unsuspecting rabbit, and the terror of the rabbit as it was taken. I felt the Earth spinning around the Sun spinning around the galaxy being blasted through infinite space and I lost all scale and orientation, the void inside me diffusing tracelessly into the void outside me and I was everything and I was nothing at all.

I had no boundaries and no limits. Any number divided by infinity = zero. Just stand here and let "I" boil away like steam in the heat of enlightenment.

Gryka, still whooping, tackled me to the ground, forcefully jamming my awareness back into my body. Mostly, anyway. I was rolling around in the dirt with a hysterical predator, I had just lost absolutely everything that defined me, and the realization caused me to sob with mingled shame and relief—like watching your house burn, but secretly being glad that you'll never have to fix the leaky roof or the crumbling foundation.

In retaliation for the tackle, I slapped her across the muzzle like a disobedient dog, hard enough to make spittle fly. Her eyes widened in disbelief for a moment—and then she threw her head back, yipping and howling and shaking even more violently than before. I grabbed onto her like I was drowning, and we cackled and whooped together for what could have been minutes or hours until the storm left us both gasping like beached fish.

Mostly left us, anyway. I allowed myself a quick moment of introspection: my soul was still gone, and a horrible, sucking black vortex of nothingness was still in its place. I realized that I now understood the gnolls as well as any human ever could or would, that I could still "see" and "hear" things I should have no way of perceiving—and that it would do me absolutely no good at all.

"*Kazhda*," I said to Gryka.

A huge grin slowly split her muzzle.

"*Hazrah nachti*," she replied.

The laughter took us again.

Aidan

———

Since Gryka came and went on her own schedule, and there was no entertainment to speak of in such a small, distant village—the major events were the arrival of trading caravans, and everything on them was available back home in Sostis for one-quarter the price—I had plenty of free time to think. I passed many a long, hot, dusty afternoon drinking a cup or two of bad coffee at the tables just outside the inn, a practice they tolerated due to a complete lack of other customers.

It was refreshing, actually, after the constant noise and interruptions of the city, to simply let my thoughts wander lazily around my head, like goldfish in a bowl. There was plenty of time to chase ideas, should any happen by.

After yesterday's episode with Gryka, I realized that I had abandoned any pretense of scholarly detachment and objectivity. Instead of treating Gryka and her pack like fragile museum exhibits that might break if handled too roughly, or like experimental animals whose behaviors I would dispassionately dissect, I had started to care about her. I felt we might even be friends of a sort after sharing such an intense experience, and I wondered why I had let it happen for the first time in my career.

My first thought: unlike most of the peaceful island cultures I had studied, I wasn't afraid of breaking Gryka or her pack. Frankly, the opposite was true. For at least a week after I met her, I dribbled a little pee into my pants every time she grinned: when a seven-foot tall bipedal hyena bares a giant mouthful of teeth at you, even in jest, it's difficult not to imagine which parts of your body might fit in there (all of them) and what would happen if they did (amputation or death.) And the first time she arrived straight from a kill, I nearly panicked and ran...

—

"Aidan O'Rourke! What do you want?" she boomed in greeting as she approached—her toothy grin splitting a mask of congealing gore.

The color drained from my face and I stammered uselessly. Her muzzle was slick and bloody to the eyes, her arms were bloody to the elbows, and her absurdly cheerful greeting left me paralyzed—too scared to run or even flinch, the cold certainty of death knotting my stomach, blood retreating into my feet.

She loped right up to me. "Why so pale?" she asked, grinning right in my face, little clots still clinging to her muzzle.

A long moment passed, and I somehow managed a weak smile. "L-look, Gryka, I know you're a carnivore, but it's still terrifying to see you like this. I feel like your dinner."

"Just ate!" she said, laughing. "Worry when I'm clean, hungry."

I blew out a deep breath and chuckled ruefully. "Can you at least go wash your hands, so you don't get blood all over my notes?"

She cocked her head at me for a moment—and nodded. "Yes. Are you thirsty?"

"Sure." I wasn't really sure, but my mouth was bone-dry.

"Then follow." And I ran to keep up with her as she casually loped out of town, to the stream.

Once we arrived, Gryka carefully inspected the near and far banks, stabbed her belt knife into the trunk of a small tree, and surprised me by leaping right into the water, purposely drenching me with the splash. She surfaced, laughing, and began industriously scrubbing her hands and muzzle. My stomach was still far too unsettled to think about swimming, so I walked upstream about ten paces and bent to the water to drink.

She emerged grinning, dripping, and apparently clean. "Stay away, meet at usual rock," she said, pushing me uphill— and before I could get completely out of range she shook herself, misting me with spray, wrung out her loincloth, grabbed and re-holstered her belt knife, and took off running at top speed, apparently air-drying herself.

Given the heat and dryness of the summer season, this didn't take long, and she arrived at the rock just as I did, panting and only slightly damp.

"I didn't know gnolls could swim, Gryka."

"Water is fun! Cool in summer, too. Gnolls are like hyenas, love water. Not like cats, rather lick entire body than go swimming." And she snorted with disdain.

———

It also helped that Gryka's attitude towards me was so nonchalant. Though she apparently enjoyed improving her English and helping me translate Gnollish, it was entirely on her schedule and at her sufferance. I knew without asking that I was absolutely her lowest priority, after hunting, sleeping, business with other humans, and whatever else she or her pack did day-to-day.

It was refreshing, actually, not to worry about cultural cross-contamination or scholarly detachment—almost like working with a colleague, if I ignored the fur, the teeth, the claws, and the meat breath. I didn't even have to worry about learning complex social rituals: she showed up when she wanted to, never used pleasantries or made small talk, and left without warning or excuse when she was done. And despite this complete lack of the usual social lubrication, I found myself enjoying her company.

Or perhaps because of it, I thought. We were so far outside each others' dominance hierarchy that none of the usual social signals mattered—which had to be a huge relief for Gryka, because rank in a gnoll pack is not only very strict, it is continually tested by those hoping to advance.

I slowly grinned as I realized: that was my life, too, at the University. No wonder we enjoyed each other's company so much.

That wasn't enough by itself, though. I enjoyed my work with many of my study subjects, and even admired a few, but I had never allowed myself to care about them. One cup of coffee later, a second thought floated by, one with the aura of rightness about it: the gnolls were the first culture I had studied that wasn't utterly doomed.

The continually growing human population meant it was a simple matter of time before all the other strange and beautiful tribes and nations I had studied—large or small, peaceful or warlike, human or non-human—were killed or scattered forever, their language and music and dress and traditions plowed under a homogenous, smothering, yet brutally efficient carpet of crops, pastures, mines, logging camps, and cities, differing only in unimportant details like native language and the specifics of architectural and military ornamentation. We might study them intently, we might even pretend to value their diversity instead of killing them for worshipping the wrong god, not wearing enough clothes, or just looking overly strange—but the moment the insatiable maw of the ever-growing city demands more bread and meat, out they must go, and we've got the army with the pikes and the archers and the cavalry and the knights, too bad, so sorry. It was easy to maintain detachment from my subjects when I could think of them as ghosts or zombies, unfortunate revenants who simply hadn't yet realized they were dead. Some of the tribes or races I studied were already under attack, and some of them would probably hang on for generations because their homeland was so harsh and marginal that we didn't place much value on it, but I gradually came to realize that I was documenting for posterity, not for preservation.

Until I met Gryka, and the gnolls.

True, they were losing ground in some places, and struggling almost everywhere—but they weren't doomed, not at all. They had been powerful enough until just recently to resist human expansion purely by force, and as I learned more about them by talking with Gryka, I realized that their starkly practical survival ethic might allow them to find some way to negotiate or force coexistence on the unwilling, ever-expanding human population. And despite the awkward fact that significant numbers of my ancestors' relatives had probably been killed and eaten by gnolls, I couldn't turn that fact into hatred. While their threat was very real out here, it had been generations since it endangered me or anyone else in Sostis.

What I did know was that I had spent my entire career chronicling the dying and the doomed, chiseling headstones on paper for the benefit of the few people who cared about dead things that didn't matter much. I had been thinking about cultural preservation for a long time, but the cultures I liked enough to preserve simply had no hope of survival except as little zoo exhibits, making trinkets for rich travelers to take home and show off how far away they'd made it from Sostis or Odene. So I put those thoughts out of my mind and got on with my career, which had allowed me to live comfortably and, in the grand scheme, do very little real work. My hands were uncallused, my back was unbowed—and though I lived modestly and possessed little, mild nearsightedness was the worst consequence of my academic life at an age where most laborers were coughing up parts of their lungs, losing their mind and teeth right in front of their barely-grown children, or already dead from injuries and diseases they were too hungry and exhausted to fight.

As I finished the last tepid dregs of my coffee, I decided that I would translate the Credo as best I could, enjoy the rest of my time with Gryka, and to hell with objectivity and impartiality. It didn't matter anyway. Simply asserting that a gnoll could read and write at all would cause such an uproar that my fellow academics would tear into me like a pack of starving street mongrels, no matter how impeccable my scholarship.

Frankly, I was looking forward to it. All the young, hungry beta males in my department were drunk on the sort of beautiful but wildly implausible frontier legends that you can still believe when you're young, quick, bold, and never, ever do fieldwork, and were spoiling for a fight with the old gray wolf occupying the tower office well past his prime, cautiously and boringly reporting that no, the Nyskal didn't keep the Philosopher's Stone in their underwater temple, nor did elves actually live forever or command the power of the lightning, even dark elves. I grinned, knowing that I'd eventually have to step down in favor of one of them, which was fine—but as long as the Duke saw me howling over big kills, like this one, I would remain top dog.

This old wolf's still got sharp teeth in his graying muzzle, I thought contentedly.

Mother

——

    Since Gryka never made small talk, I quickly became accustomed to completely random questions apropos of absolutely nothing. Gnoll relations with the townsfolk had warmed enough that she could actually sit with me outside the inn, and though I'm not certain that chairs were any more comfortable for her than squatting, it helped her appear more human-like to the burghers with whom the gnolls now did occasional business, so I encouraged her to use them. Even so, she never really understood the concept of paying for food, and she never entered the inn unless to speak with me. Food was something that ran away from you, and I got the strong impression (though I never asked—I should have) that having someone bring you prepared food implied that you were either sick, injured, or a nursing baby. Being none of these, she always refused.

Anyway, we were sitting on the deck, outdoors, in the shade. I was enjoying a terrible cup of coffee, black, and she asked me "Why drink that? Smells like charcoal."

I offered the cup to her. "Taste?"

She shrugged, took the cup, sniffed it, and somehow directed a moderately-sized sip into that huge, blocky muzzle without spilling or making a ridiculous noise. I was impressed.

She wrinkled her nose. "Tastes like charcoal, too. Why drink it?"

"There's something in it that makes humans both awake and relaxed at the same time, unless we drink too much. Then we stay awake, but get jittery and have to pee a lot."

"We chew a root sometimes when we need to wait a very long time in one place, not moving."

"Like fishing?"

"Yes, or hunting alone like leopard, waiting in tree. Root makes waiting easier. But if we chew too much, prey passes, we forget to chase it." She snorted.

"Do you ever chew it when not hunting? Just for fun?"

She thought about that. "No. After chewing root, talk hurts my head. Hate others, have to be alone. Also, root bad for mothers. Makes milk sour."

I wondered what root that could be. Sounded like an ibogaine equivalent...I could ask her to bring me some or show me the plant, but what I know about botany could fit on a napkin.

"I thought of something, Gryka. Most people put cream and sugar in their coffee; makes it sweeter. Would you like to try that?"

She shrugged again. "Sweet burnt charcoal. Maybe it keeps me awake if I drink more?"

My turn to shrug. I poured some cream into the remaining half-cup, spooned in some sugar, stirred it, and took an exploratory sip. Tasted like lukewarm candy to me, but I had been drinking black coffee for years.

I handed her the cup. She sniffed it and tossed back the remainder of its contents, sugar sludge and all.

Nothing could have prepared me for what happened next. She went completely catatonic, eyes still open and staring at me, but totally unseeing. Her hand, and the empty coffee cup with it, fell to her side, whereupon the cup dropped to the wooden deck. She was taking short, quick, shallow breaths. If I had believed it were possible, I would have said she was having a panic attack.

"Gryka?" My voice came out quieter than I intended, and a little bit squeaky.

No response.

"Gryka?" I sounded better, but it didn't help. She was breathing faster and faster, practically panting.

Was caffeine poisonous to gnolls? What the hell was going on? "Gryka!" I wanted to grab her arm, but they were by her sides and I couldn't reach either one from my seat across the table. I got up, stepped over to her, looked into her glassy, unseeing eyes, and shook her shoulder. "GRYKA!"

My world exploded in a deafening scream as Gryka sprang from her chair and smacked me clear off the deck with a flailing palm strike. Pain seared my shoulder, the world spun around me, I landed in the dirt, and passed out.

I must have come back to consciousness fairly quickly,

because I could see the cobblestones of a side street whizzing through my field of vision, bottom to top. Someone had me in a fireman's carry—someone who moved very, very quickly—someone with yellow, spotted fur and a black-tipped tail.

"Gryka?" The cobbles changed abruptly to dirt.

"Gryka! What the hell!" I was afraid to struggle. If she dropped me at the speed we were moving, it would be like falling off a horse face-first.

The dirt changed to grass. I saw shadows, and smelled water. "Look, Gryka, put me down, okay? Just put me down and tell me what the hell just happened."

She put me down. I was able to stand, though I was a bit wobbly, and my shoulder sizzled with pain. I looked at it and hissed...my shirt was shredded, and blood was welling out of four parallel claw gouges and flowing down my arm. I could move my arm and my hand, but those were some deep, bad cuts, and I was losing a lot of blood, fast.

"Fix this now. Sit." She slapped a rock next to her.

I was in too much shock to do anything else; so I sat.

She sliced my shirt away from me with those same short but wickedly sharp claws. (I later learned that she kept them razor-sharp with a small stone she kept on her belt. Most gnolls just used rocks, but Gryka was fastidious about this. "The difference between fighting prey and dead prey, maybe.")

Then she pulled my arm up to a right angle away from my torso, to the side ("Keep cuts shut") and licked the blood off my arm and shoulder with the flat of her huge, rough tongue. "So easy," she said, "no fur. Now hold your arm there."

She bent to the stream, scooped up some water in her hands, and dumped the cool water over my shoulder, repeating this several times. Blood kept welling out of the cuts and down my torso. I was starting to feel faint.

She exhaled, with a very human "hrmph" sound. "This will stink, but you lose too much blood now."

As far as I could tell, she wiped her hand on her ass and came back with a tarry, incredibly stinky goop on her fingers. "What the HELL, Gryka?" Are the gnolls one of those primitive tribes that rubs shit on wounds? I was ready to run, blood loss or no; I'd take that risk any day over certain sepsis.

"No, no, no, not shit. Scent glands. Stinks, but dries up skin, stops bleeding."

Oh, no.

"We clean again later. You lose more blood now, you pass out."

I'm not shy of leeches or needles, but I couldn't watch her rub that stuff on me. It looked like greasy, half-dried diarrhea and smelled like...even my best words fail me. Like six hundred skunks fucking, maybe, in a cart full of rotting mangoes, in the sun. In July. Garnish with a dead zebra and some ground coffee, puke some bile on top of it, and add a really disturbing top note of vanilla. You still can't imagine how nauseating it smelled, but I'm absolutely not kidding about the vanilla. It made everything else so much worse. The entire rest of my life, I've never had to restrain myself from overindulgence; I just imagine that smell again and instantly lose my appetite.

The worst thing was that I knew I wasn't going to barf—I was just going to think about it constantly for the next few hours. I gritted my teeth and tried to breathe through my mouth as she smeared the evil butt grease on my shoulder, which didn't take long.

It didn't feel like anything at all, at least not right away. My shoulder looked like it had shit smeared on it, but to my surprise, the bleeding had almost entirely stopped. I could already see the skin crinkling around the edges of the slashes.

Gryka grinned at me. "You want fast, easy way, or no scars?"

"What do you mean?"

"Put arm down now, I put more butter on it, stop bleeding, can use arm fast, big scars. Leave arm up until cuts heal shut, maybe...two days for you, little scars."

The bleeding had completely stopped. Apparently the "butter" (that association ruined real butter for me, for weeks) was a powerful desiccant, clotting agent, or whatever—I'm not a physician, but it worked.

I thought about my choice for a while. Two days? I couldn't go back to town smelling like a gnoll's ass...but I couldn't hold my arm up for two days, either, and I smelled like a gnoll's ass already. "Screw it, chicks dig scars."

She cocked her head, puzzled. Too idiomatic.

I tried again. "Put my arm down and do it. Women like scars, right?"

She laughed. "Yes, but only a few. Too many means you're clumsy. Need good stories, too. Breathe now."

"What?" She put my arm down, and I hissed as the cuts opened again. Even worse, she was working the evil grease inside the cuts. I clenched my fists and growled in pain.

"Done now. Hold this." She gave me one side of my mutilated shirt to hold, stretched it taut, sliced off the cleanest piece with her claws, quickly folded it, and put it in my good hand. "Now hold over cuts."

I slapped it over my bad shoulder and held it there firmly.

"Good. Keep butter in, maybe twenty minutes. Stay here, I find place for you tonight."

"Wait, Gryka. I need to at least tell the innkeeper that I'm alive, because the last thing he saw was you attacking me and carrying my body out to the forest. As soon as the townsfolk get drunk enough to be brave, they'll send out a search party, maybe with dogs. I don't want any of us to get hurt."

She thought for several seconds. "Yes. Can you walk?"

"Let me try." I stood up and took a few steps. "Maybe a block, no more."

"Then I carry you back to town, drop you near inn. Wait for you, carry you back."

"What if someone finds you while you're waiting?"

She snorted.

"They're all scared of you, but they'll still kill you if they can. Stay safe."

The trip into town and back actually went well, for a change. The innkeeper rushed over to me, disbelieving that I was alive, but the stink kept him at a distance—as it did the rest of the rapidly gathering crowd. Given the smell and the wounds on my shoulder, I'm sure they thought I killed Gryka with some unfathomable magic—and I wasn't above using the unearned fear and respect to get a change of clothes and a sack of sandwiches brought to me. I told them I needed some time to reflect on what happened, I'd be back in a few days, don't follow me, and strode confidently back to Gryka's hiding place, collapsing at her feet. She picked me up, threw me over her shoulder again, tucked my clothes in her belt, held the sack in her free hand, and I closed my eyes for the bumpy ride to...wherever she was taking me. I had no more energy to assume any responsibility for myself.

Gryka put me down in the mouth of a small hillside cave, just tall enough at the entrance to stand up in, with a breath-taking view of the sun low in the sky over distant mountains. It would be a beautiful sunset, I thought, and I sat against the wall to watch it.

She looked at my shoulder with a critical eye. "Cuts not dangerous, just painful," she said. "Big arteries on inside, under arm."

More surprises. "You know anatomy?"

"What is anatomy?"

"Where things are inside a body."

I realized I had just answered my own question. She snorted at me anyway. "Meat is our life, Aidan. We know where everything is, inside. First thing to learn as cub, the tasty parts, to eat first. Then the weak parts, to hunt. Then everything else."

It hit me that not only had gnolls killed countless humans over the centuries, Gryka had probably killed humans herself —and then eaten them. Suddenly I was very glad she was my friend. Her ineffectual, slapping strike—just a startle reflex, really—had come within a few inches of tearing my arm off.

"Gryka, is there anything in this cave?"

I saw a quick and totally unfamiliar expression cross her face, and she growled quietly to herself.

"Don't know. You wait outside, I look."

I got up and walked around the corner. This could be interesting. Should I try to find a weapon? Then I realized: anything that could take out Gryka, even in the dark, was nothing I could handle without a phalanx of well-armed bodyguards. I sat down to await events.

It didn't take long. There was a sudden cacophony of grunts and shrieks, and a cloud of little javelinas exploded from the cave mouth. Soon after, Gryka emerged, grinning widely, with two wriggling, squealing little bundles, one in each hand. "Dinner! Want some?"

I couldn't imagine how she was holding onto them...and then I remembered her claws. "Only if you want to build a fire for me. I've got sandwiches."

"Why not?" she asked. "Build fire, watch sunset, eat pigs, sleep."

So we did.

"Gryka?"

She grunted.

"I'm freezing." It was a clear night, the upward and outward-sloping ceiling wasn't trapping any heat, and once the fire burned down to coals, it was actually fairly chilly in the cave. Plus I was sleeping—or trying to sleep—on a stone cave floor in summer clothes. I was shivering so hard my teeth were chattering.

"Cold too. Come here." She patted the ground in front of her.

One more step into the void, I thought. But what choice did I have? Shivering all night and no sleep?

I laid down next to her, and snuggled up to her big, bony, warm, furry body. With gnolls, female spoons *you*, I thought to myself.

"You stink worse than I do," she rumbled.

"Whose fault is that?" I reminded her. "Besides, you never did tell me what happened to you today." Her internal furnace ran hot: I wasn't shivering any more.

"Talk tomorrow. Sleep now." She threw a furry arm over me, and as far as I could tell by her regular breathing, fell asleep immediately.

And, apparently, so did I.

We awoke the next day to a luminous false dawn, the sky slowly shifting through a beautiful palette of subtle brushed-metal gray-blues. I yawned, stretched, and went out front to piss, and was just unbuttoning when Gryka called out "Wait.

Go farther."

"Why?"

"Piss marks territory. Keeps pigs out."

"Gryka, it's going to smell like your ass in there for weeks. You'll be lucky if the pigs come back before winter." I pulled out my cock and wrote my name in the dirt, "Aidan" in big looping script. I didn't have enough in the tank to start on "O'Rourke", so I added an underline, tapped off, buttoned up, and went back inside.

Gryka was still on the floor, looking sleepy. "Early, still cold. Keep me warm." She patted the ground next to herself.

I put my hands on my hips and tried to look stern. "I thought predators were supposed to get up early and hunt during these fertile crepuscular hours. Early bird gets the worm, and all that. Plus, you still owe me an explanation for yesterday."

"Ate two pigs last night. Not hungry. Warm me up, then I talk."

"Not fair. You can eat a whole sheep at once and not be hungry for most of a week. I can't eat enough in an entire day not to be hungry the next morning. Let me take a couple bites of this sandwich first."

That done, I snuggled up next to her again. It was warm and pleasant, I had to admit, and still cold out...the sky was barely pinkish. "Shoulder looks good," she rumbled. "Big scabs, not too red." She threw a long, lanky arm over me again.

"I hope so, but it still feels like hot bees in there. Now tell me: what the hell happened yesterday, after you drank that coffee?"

She sighed. "Coffee, sugar, milk. Coffee tastes like charcoal, yes?"

"Not to me, really, but I understand the similarity."

"To me, charcoal. Burnt. After a fire. And warm, sweet milk. Mother's milk."

A pause.

"I was tiny. Not weaned yet. Mother is big, warm, furry, everything. Her teats are the best thing, the only thing. I killed my sister so I would have one to myself."

She must have felt my surprise. "Born fighting. Teeth, claws, eyes open. You didn't know?"

"I knew many died; I didn't know why."

"Other things too. Anyway, cubs stay in tunnels, mostly. Safer. Big animals can't get in, even adults can't. Whole world just for little cubs."

Another pause.

"Little gnoll cubs too small to attack big animals. They go back, and back, and back, back into tunnel, always slashing at nose or paws of big animal trying to eat them. Later we learn to hunt, but as sucking cub, we know only...instinct, yes?"

"Yes, instinct."

She paused, and sighed again.

"Then, a fire."

I realized I didn't like where this was going. At all. But I wasn't going anywhere, lying spooned on the floor with her arm around me.

"Tunnels usually in grassland. Ours in forest, that time. Don't know why. Anyway, fire. It was windy, I think. Fire moved fast."

I felt her muscles tense slightly.

"Fire snaps and cracks and roars, like predator. Bright, flashing. Scared. Go back, back, back into tunnel. Hide." She gripped my arm, hard.

"Mother came for me. Called to me. I wanted to go to her, but couldn't see her. The fire snapped and roared, louder and louder. Mother reached down the tunnel to grab me, but I was too scared, too little, too scared..." She was quivering now, crushing me to her.

"I slashed! I slashed and I howled at the huge, clawed hand reaching for me! I could smell Mother, but this huge hand kept trying to take me, and I kept slashing at it, howling, slashing, howling, and I could hear Mother howling too and I was so scared, so scared, so tiny and scared..." Gryka shook and hugged me harder, but with no strength at all, breathing tiny little useless breaths.

"Fire snapped and roared, louder, louder, and attacked! The ground shook, dirt rained on me, and the hand snapped at me in one last desperate attack as I slashed, slashed, slashed for my life, and the hand finally stopped but the howling turned to screaming and got even louder and worse and I was so scared, so scared, so tiny and scared..."

"Finally the screaming stopped, and the fire was still snapping, but more quietly now, and there is not much in a cub's mind but it came back, a little. It was hot and sleepy in that tunnel, so I went around to a different one, looked out. Lots of fire and everything smelled funny, so I stayed down for a while until it got quieter. Then I poked my head out and I could see Mother, so it was fine." Her breathing was irregular and she was convulsively squeezing me, kneading me with her hands and limbs like a gigantic cat.

Oh, no. I knew exactly what had happened now. A big, fat widowmaker had fallen from a burning tree and crushed Gryka's mother while she was trying to pull her tiny, still-nursing child out of the tunnels. One-in-a-million shot by that damned tree. Gnolls are tough, tough beasts, but a big enough branch falling from high enough could probably take one out.

And Gryka was going to relive it with me trapped in

her grasp. Here we go, I thought. I hope at least one of us survives this.

"I went through the smoking, burning stuff to my mother. Everything was fine once I could see her. I pulled on her leg and yipped, like I did when I wanted a teat, but she didn't move, so I climbed over her to take one, and her fur was black and crusty and smelled wrong..."

She was kneading, kneading, kneading me and shivering with big, convulsive shudders.

"I was hungry, so I suckled her anyway, with the charcoal taste of burnt fur in my mouth..."

Bad black coffee, cream, sugar. Burnt fur and mother's milk. And here we are.

"I got some milk, but then...then..."

Oh, no.

"...then her nipple came off in my mouth, and even as a tiny cub I knew that was wrong, and I scrambled over to her head. The huge branch had fallen across her as she reached for me..."

"...but that didn't kill her, it crushed her spine and paralyzed her. The howling I heard after the branch fell..."

No, no, no. This was worse than anything I could have imagined, ever.

"was Mother... paralyzed... burning... screaming... screaming..."

I lost it, totally, completely. She had pulled me so far into her reality that I howled with her pain, loss, and guilt, guilt and regret, an endless, lifeless, steel-gray ocean of pain and loss under an endless gray sky of guilt, and she howled and crushed me to her like I could save her, and we were two drowning people each trying to push the other down to stay above water and we howled and shook and sobbed and screamed like dying animals and there was no transcendence or mystical experience or even the tiniest scrap of solace here, just two mindless, dying animals on the cold floor of a cave.

Some endless time later, I came back to my senses, still on the cave floor, tangled up with Gryka. The sun had long since risen and the air was getting warm.

I felt weak, shaky, threadbare and wrung out, like an old, cheap washcloth. My shoulder still hurt and the scabs were weeping a few threads of pus and blood, but everything else seemed to still be attached. I flopped myself over so I could see Gryka's face.

Our eyes met. "You look like shit," I said, and it was true. She looked haggard and spent, like a shipwreck survivor. Her facial fur was streaked with dirt and tears, her eyes were red, bloodshot, and unfocused, her ruff was matted and crushed, and her tongue hung slightly out of her mouth.

She cocked an eye at me just the slightest fraction. "You look worse."

I probably did, but I wasn't going to let that one get by me. "Worse than shit? What looks worse than shit?"

"You."

I had no hands free, so I headbutted her muzzle, very lightly.

She grinned, a little. "Don't make me bite you."

"Or laugh. Or move. Ouch." That headbutt was a mistake.

Some time passed. We stared at each other, finding nothing to say. Finally:

"Gryka?"

"Aidan?"

"Stand up, okay?" She did.

I put my hands on her shoulders. "Do we have to do that again, ever? Because I can't take it. I really can't. I don't know how you live with it, and I'm amazed that you have, because

I couldn't, but I can't take that again, even second-hand."

She gave me the saddest smile I've ever seen on anyone, human or gnoll, tears shining in the corners of her eyes. "No, Aidan. Neither of us has to do that again. Ever."

I gave her, I think, my own sad smile.

"Aidan...?"

I'd never before heard her start a thought without finishing it.

"Sometimes I wish you were a gnoll."

I started crying again and buried my face in her chest, soaking it with tears. "Oh, goddamnit, Gryka, that's the nicest thing anyone has said to me. Ever." I picked my head up and fixed her with my stare again, hands still on her shoulders. "Do you believe that?"

The tears dripped silently down her muzzle as she nodded. "Yes."

"*Kazhda,* right?"

She nodded again. "*Kazhda.*"

"Then believe me when I say this. Somewhere, sometime, somehow, there is a place and time where what we both wish is true for both of us. Maybe the world has to die and be reborn again. Maybe it has to happen a million times, maybe a billion times, maybe just again and again and again until it gets it fucking right, okay? Maybe it already happened and we'll never know. Maybe it'll happen both ways, and every other way, over and over again and we'll never know. But someday, somewhere, sometime, *it happens.* And if you think the ocean of the dead is endless, it's a speck of exactly zero size in the big black universe of what might have happened, and I don't care at all, because somewhere out there, there is at least One. Single. Place. where we both get our wish, right?" I was so angry, and crying so hard, that I could barely grind the words out.

She nodded, silent tears flowing.

And just as quickly, the storm was over. I scowled.

"No, it's probably bullshit, and if it isn't, we'll never know. *Hazrah nachti.* It is what it is, we've got what we've got, here, now. But you know what?"

She looked stricken, like I had convinced her and pulled the rug back out.

"It's still worth it. I lied before. I'd do it again, for you. I can swallow that fire and laugh, for you. See? I'm laughing right now." And I was. The endless hungry black void inside me can take any pain, any joy, any triumph, any sadness, put out any fire, again and again, without being measurably filled or diminished. That is its power and its gift, and I gloried in it as the laughter surged up and took both of us away from pain, away from loss, an end to our endless sadness.

———

Some time later: "You know why I slashed you that day, right?"

"I think so. The memory from the coffee turned you back into a cub, right?"

"Yes. I was a little cub, backing up and slashing, backing up and slashing."

"I'm glad cubs don't bite."

"They bite, but only other cubs." She grinned.

How long was I going to play this dangerous game? My guess: until one of us died. And I was right.

Names

——

I tried quite a few times, but I never did get the Gnollish pronunciation of Gryka's name quite right. This didn't bother her; as far as she was concerned, her name to her packmates was a completely different word than her name to humans, and neither defined her. "I don't need a name for myself," she said to me once. "I give a name for others to use."

"How did you get your name, Gryka? Did you choose it?"

"No, Mother gave it to me."

"I don't understand."

She thought for a moment. "When I was a cub, 'Gryka' just meant 'Mother wants you.' Now it means 'The one who speaks wants you.' I could throw Gryka away and choose another name, but it still means 'The one who speaks wants you.'"

"Do gnoll names mean anything?"

She thought for another, longer moment. I was used to these long pauses when talking with her; she never said anything before she was ready. I admired this and still try to emulate it, with limited success; it's hard to break the habit of filling up every conversational silence with words, even if they're not important and mean nothing.

"No, just easy to say."

I guess that's why they're all two syllables and sound like the growling *whoop* of a hyena. Purely functional. I was jealous.

"It's very different for humans. Names all mean something."

Another pause. "Explain."

"It's not the same for everyone, but I'll talk about my culture. You know most of us have two names, right? First and last, given and family?"

She nodded.

"The last name is easy, it's the family name. We take ours from the father." She snorted. "Yes, I know that makes no sense to you. We could take it from the mother, it doesn't really matter. Either way, our last name always comes from our parents."

"I know."

"But it was different, before. People used to take the last name of their job, or maybe where they were from. Butcher, Miller, Smith, Fisher, Baker, Shepard, Washington, Hamilton, ... but since people take the name of their fathers now, most Butchers aren't butchers anymore, most Millers aren't millers anymore...a Fisher is as likely to be a shepherd as a fisherman!"

She kept looking at me intently, so I went on. "Well, here's the problem. What sort of person is a blacksmith?"

"Big, strong, hits iron with hammer all day, sweats a lot."

I laughed. "Right. And what sort of person is a shepherd?"

"Quiet, likes being alone, likes sheep, maybe too much, stupid."

I laughed again. "So what happens now, four or five generations later, when the Smiths are shepherds, the Shepards are blacksmiths, the Butchers are millers, the Bakers go fishing, and the Hamiltons move to Dolhin?" By this point I was laughing so hard at her crack about shepherds that I barely got the last words out.

Gryka howled with laughter and pounded the table with her big, blocky fists, and her laugh was so infectious that I lost it too. There was probably a drinking song or some dirty limericks in here somewhere, if I ever took the time to try. "There once was a fisher named Smith..."

I almost started back in with birth names, but Gryka was still giggling, and why rush the moment? Good, strong belly laughs don't come every day, and I was happy to finally share one with her that didn't involve washing blood out of my clothes and hair afterward.

Finally her giggles wound down to a lopsided look of grinning skepticism. "Aidan O'Rourke. Clan of hill kings?"

"I doubt any of my ancestors ever ruled more than a cow and some chickens."

She nodded, still grinning. "More, yes?"

"Right, the given name, which is what most people call us. The story's not as funny, but probably worse for us. Our parents pick one for us before we're born..." At that, Gryka's expression registered surprise. "Actually they pick two, since they don't know whether it'll be a boy or a girl. We only have one at a time, usually, and more of them survive than do yours."

She nodded.

"But why do parents pick a given name? Often just because it sounds nice, or because a famous person has it, but usually it's because of something they want their child to be when he or she grows up."

She still wore a look of earnest puzzlement.

"But *how do they know that?*" I demanded. "How do they know what the child will be like? If you name a baby Timothy, will he grow up to serve God? Will Erik be the single ruler, or Henry the home ruler? Will Felix be lucky or Edward rich? Will Roger be a *famous spear thrower?* What if Roger becomes a farmer, Timothy a drunk, Henry a sailor, and Edward a monk?" I shook my head and winced: unintentional doggerel was tacky.

"I see the problem. Easier for gnolls, we're all the same."

"Which is why I'm glad you don't try to make your names mean something, or you'd all sound like orcs. Bonecrusher, Shieldbreaker, Skullhammer..."

She whooped. "Darkclaw! Sharptooth! Whitefang! Quickpaw! Put words in two stacks, pick one from each!"

My jaw dropped. She got the joke, and the meta-joke even most humans never got. I loved her, but was glad she wasn't in my department, competing for publishing credit or the chairmanship.

The mental picture was so ridiculous that I whooped, too. I pictured her stalking the dais in front of a crowd of quaking freshmen, naked but for her usual weapon belt and tiny loincloth, gore up to her eyes and elbows, roaring about subjective perception while shoving bowls of chives, glazed lamb chops, and rotting, maggoty offal in their waxy, terrified faces as they pissed themselves one by one...I pointed at her and collapsed entirely with laughter.

She was still going, howling and pounding the table with each new name. "Brightmane! Swiftfoot! Keeneye! SPIIIIINECRACKERRRRR!"

It was a good night, maybe the best. One of them, anyway. I waved at her as she loped away into the night, both of us still giggling.

Meat

—

The next summer, I rented a house at the edge of town instead of staying at the inn. It had a small porch and balcony on its north side, onto which I could escape when the air was too still to cool the indoors, and most importantly, a stove and butcher block—and though my cooking wins no awards, it was cheaper than eating every meal at the inn, even when I just heated up food someone else had made.

I tossed Gryka a can from the top of the stack. "Can you open this? I can't find a single can opener in this entire damned house."

She turned it over in her hands and smelled it. "What's inside?"

"Beef stew."

She popped the entire can into her mouth.

I raised one eyebrow and grinned. "Good one. Does that belt knife of yours open cans?"

In response, she bit down. Dumbfounded, I heard metal crunch and snap.

Gryka chewed slowly and with great concentration, swallowed, and spat two mangled shreds of metal to the floor. "Tastes good, but too many vegetables. I go hunt."

And with that, she left.

My exhaustive search for can-opening tools yielded a horseshoe, a hand axe, some rusty nails—and, finally, a hammer and chisel. I built a small fire in the stove, sat at the table, and waited for Gryka to return. Just before sunset, she bounced through the doorway, hands and muzzle red with fresh blood, eyes sparkling, brandishing a small but complete antelope haunch.

"Fawn! Young, tender, delicious! I saved some for you." She tossed the entire bloody, ragged haunch to me in a slow, underhand arc.

Oh, hell, I thought. But what could I do, really? I caught it, splashing myself, my clothes, and the floor with blood. It was still warm with the heat of life.

It smelled delicious.

I brought it closer to my nose and inhaled deeply. The smell was more than delicious, it was intoxicating. Butcher shops don't smell like this, I thought, and abattoirs are just disgusting. Has freshly killed wild game always smelled like this and I just never knew it, or have I been spending too much time with Gryka? What's happening to me?

She said nothing, watching me intently but impassively.

I surrendered to the impulse, buried my face in the exposed muscle, and tried to take a bite. My nose got in the way, and my teeth had problems—fresh meat, even from the very young, is extremely tough, and I had to saw back and forth with my incisors to worry off a chunk even after Gryka's teeth had already ripped the muscle halfway apart—but I finally tore off a big, solid bite.

I can still taste that single mouthful. Warm, salty, musky, wild, and damn near impossible to chew. It took me a full minute for my molars to smash it down into something I could swallow. Even then, the lump was too big, and it painfully distended my throat as it went down.

Gryka was grinning at me, that big, toothy, lopsided grin I grew to understand as well as anyone ever would, still bloody to the forearms and eyes. I grinned back, sitting in that silly little wooden chair, gore up to my own eyes, hardly-diminished haunch dripping on my lap and onto the floor.

"Thanks, Gryka."

I tossed the haunch over to one side, up onto the butcher block, and immediately lost myself in sadness. The deep, ancient memory of my blood sang to me: This is right, this is what you are, this is what you do, this is how you live. Keep eating. But my weak, flabby, human body just couldn't do it. My teeth can't even break hide, let alone crush bone like Gryka's, and they can barely gnaw through the tenderest fresh meat. My claws are soft, thin, and useless for anything but painting decorations on.

I thought: we humans are slow and weak for our size, and need all the tools we can make, buy, or steal just to stay alive. They weigh us down. We can't go anywhere without several pounds of tools and clothes slapping and flapping about us, like a boat dragging its anchors in the water behind it, and since we need a different tool to do everything and we can't carry them all even if we wanted to, we have to build houses to store the ones we're not using, and locks and police to stop other people from taking them when we're not home, and pretty soon we've got laws, courts, jails, politics, governments, armies, the entire stifling superstructure of civilization—all because we're too weak to kill and eat other animals with our own hands and teeth.

"*Kazhda.* I hate my ancestors, Gryka."

She listened intently but said nothing.

"They traded all their strength, all their speed, all their power away for these big goddamned brains," I tapped my head, "and all our brains do is make us unhappy by remembering the things we could do if we hadn't."

She cocked her head, thinking, for a long time. Neither of us said anything.

"You live, yes?" she asked.

I spread my hands and shrugged. "Guilty." I don't think she got the joke.

"I think it is much easier to be dead than alive."

"So?"

"Most children die. How many baby rabbits grow into jacks, and how many are eaten by the fox, the hyena, the hawk, the owl?"

"Most of them. Rabbits are famous for having lots of baby rabbits, and if they didn't get eaten, we'd all be up to our asses in rabbits. We'd have to go live on boats."

Gryka laughed. "And how many jacks find a mate, fuck her, dig burrow, feed her, keep her safe until babies come? How many are eaten first?"

"A lot of them."

"So, more dead rabbits than living rabbits. Many more."

"Well, yes."

She stopped to think a while longer.

"Living rabbits are faster than dead rabbits."

I made a face at her. "Of course. Even I can catch a dead rabbit."

"No. Living rabbits are faster than dead rabbits were before they died. That is why they live and dead ones die."

I was dumbfounded. Gryka was reverse-engineering the theory of natural selection, right in front of me. Or did the gnolls already understand it?

"So your ancestors all lived, found a mate, made children, and you are here now. The others are all dead, or never lived."

"Oh, hell, I know that, Gryka."

"No, you don't." I had never seen her angry before, and was shocked into silence by her stern rebuke. "So many dead people. Killed by bison or snakes or lions or gnolls. Killed by winter cold or summer heat. Killed by pox or shakes or croup or sleeping sickness or fever. Killed by bad plants that look like good plants. Killed by bandits, killed by war, drowned in the river, starved by drought or bad kings. All dead. *You live.*"

She kept going. "No more big-tooth cats, no more hairy elephants, no more cave hyenas, no more dire wolves, no more giant lizards. No more giant tree sloths, we ate them. All dead. *You live.*"

I had never seen Gryka like this, and frankly, I was too terrified to understand. She grabbed me by the shirt, yanked me to my feet, and pulled my face close to hers. Her hot breath washed my face as she hissed the words with a terrible, quiet intensity:

"We say *'hazrah nachti'* and we laugh, because *we live to say it.* Do you understand?"

At that moment, I finally accepted that Gryka was going to kill and eat me, and I would lose my years-long gamble of associating closely with climax predators well-known for eating humans, ending up as a humorous footnote, like the man who lived with polar bears and finally got eaten by one, just like everyone said would happen. And as my fear drained away and was replaced by calm acceptance, the words which had been bouncing off my fear finally sank in.

Each and every one of us sits, stands, walks, runs, eats, fucks, works, plays, and sleeps atop a giant pile of rotting corpses. What is dirt? Shit, rocks, and the dead. So many dead. Endless dead. Our ancestors form a colossal pyramid of dead people, with each of us at the apex, but those billions of macabre corpse-pyramids are themselves submerged within the endless screaming ocean of corpses that failed to become ancestors, all the way to the unfathomably distant horizon at the beginning of time.

Soon enough, I would be joining them.

But meanwhile, I had some things to do. "*Kazhda.* Gryka, put me down. I need to cook dinner."

She cocked one eye at me but didn't grin...and didn't put me down.

"Seriously, I understand. You're right, it's astounding that we're here at all, considering the odds and the alternatives. But sometimes—and especially just now, when you tossed me that antelope shank—I really wish that I were a gnoll, too."

She looked at me quizzically for a moment, then put me down. Then she hugged me so hard it drove the breath from my lungs.

More Meat

———

One day I met Gryka at my usual place in the village square. Or, rather, she met me, as she usually did, being more able than I to travel long distances, without roads, in short times, for little or no reason.

"Aidan O'Rourke. What do you want?" she boomed, as she always did. She sounded joyously happy but was walking slowly, with less of her usual bounce. And she looked...bigger. Heavier. Almost...fat. No, really fat. Her limbs were of normal size, but she looked like she had gained about eighty pounds overnight. (And as it turned out, my guess was right on.)

"Gryka! Are you pregnant?" In all my time with her, I

never once managed to offend her by asking a too-personal question. Sometimes she would simply not answer, but I never ran into the equivalent of a cultural taboo, and I don't recall a question ever angering her.

"I just ate an impala!"

Finally she ambled close enough for both of us to stop yelling. "Who cares? You eat impala all the time."

"The entire impala!" She belched cheerfully.

It turns out that gnolls, like hyenas, can eat up to a third of their body weight. It also turns out that a small impala ram weighs about eighty pounds once you barf up the hooves, the horns, and the fur.

"Why don't you just eat all that stuff? You eat everything else, and it's not like you can't chew them."

"Comes out the back end the same. Also, tastes like wood."

"I didn't know gnolls cared what things tasted like."

She cuffed me—lightly by her standards, but it would leave a mark—and gave me one of her rare but pungent snorts of disdain.

"Then how do you eat carrion and all that other disgusting crap?" I asked.

"You eat beef?"

"Of course." I slapped my stomach, burped up some lunch —steak, potatoes, gravy—and blew it at her. She laughed.

"Butcher hangs meat. Why?"

"So you know he's the butcher. If there isn't any meat in the window, how would you know to go in?"

"No, lots more in back. Why?"

"He's smoking it? Making pastrami or jerky?"

"No. That steak you eat, butcher has for week, maybe more. Why?"

I gave up. "You tell me. Why?"

"Must rot first. More tender, tastes better."

I cuffed her back. "Bullshit!"

She grinned hugely. "Tastes much better. Ask butcher yourself." So I did.

———

Gryka was right: the longer you can "age" beef before it turns moldy or maggoty, the better it tastes. I guess I shouldn't have been surprised: I can cut a nearly-raw Delmonico with a fork, but I could barely rip a piece out of that raw fawn's haunch she gave me with all the strength in my jaws.

I thought about this for a while. When I next saw her, two days later, she looked substantially skinnier. I would ask about that later, but right now I had a more pressing question.

"I asked the butcher, and you're right. Beef tastes better when it rots longer. The problem is, eventually it rots so much it makes us sick, and when that happens, it starts to taste really bad."

"Go other way around. If rotten meat didn't taste bad to humans, humans would eat rotten meat, get sick. Doesn't make gnolls sick." Gryka grinned.

Oh, no. I was beginning to understand. "So when you dig into that rotten corpse, maggots, blowflies, fungus, and all, it's like pastrami or dry-aged tenderloin to us."

"Tastes great to gnolls. More flavor, more tender. Maggots taste good too, like if walnuts had brains." Her eyes glittered, and I think she even drooled a little.

Once again, I was just about to understand something profound about gnolls that would never do me any damn good. "Gryka, I was going to get you some absolutely first-class human food to see if you could tell the difference, but I think I understand the problem. If you can eat carrion and enjoy it, everything humans eat has to seem weak and insipid to you, like nothing at all."

She thought about this for a moment, and nodded. "Also, too many vegetables. Vegetables aren't food for us."

"What do they taste like, though?"

"Nothing. Like not-food. Do you eat grass?"

"No..." Oh. I imagined a dinner plate with a tiny, utterly flavorless piece of poached whitefish on it, surrounded by neat piles of various types and species of cut grass, and laughed out loud.

Then I felt a stab of jealousy. I realized I could easily publish a book on the Subjective Nature of Perception, based entirely on the insights Gryka casually dropped on me in two brief conversations about food. How does a savage half-human, who spends most of her time sleeping and chasing prey animals, and will likely die in useless, violent tribal conflict, understand so much using only her limited experience? I was literally one more effortless insight away from resigning my professorship by mail, finding the nearest order of contemplative monks, and joining it...

...but I had to ask her, first.

"Gryka, when we talk like this, I always learn so much from you that it makes me feel like you're smart and I'm stupid. What do you think?"

She replied without hesitation. "I only think like this when I am with you. When I am with my pack, hunting, meat, children, territory. I am happy, but I do not think of new things."

"Tonight, though. None of this was new to you. You taught me about meat. I didn't teach you anything."

"So many things I know, but cannot say. When I talk to you, I must say them. Difficult, but fun. Like hunting prey in head."

She paused, and grinned. "Also, I cheat. Gnolls know more

about meat than anyone. Meat is our life. Next time I ask you about cities, and you talk."

Had I been talking to anyone else, I would have suspected condescension—but I had never known Gryka to be anything but brutally honest with me. Suddenly I felt much better about my academic qualifications.

I had one last question. "You're a lot skinnier than when I saw you two days ago. Did you really digest thirty pounds of meat in two days?"

"Lots of hide and bone, comes out quick," she said, with a huge, goofy, lopsided grin. "Also, eating for four."

This time, it was my turn to cuff her. "You said you weren't pregnant!"

"I wasn't. Was that night." Still grinning, she let her huge tongue dangle, and panted in an instantly recognizable parody of lust.

"Congratulations!" I hugged her, hard. "Wait...how the hell do you know already?"

"We know right away. Don't you?"

Terrible memories of my divorce stirred from the mucky depths and began to surface. "No, Gryka. No, we don't." Damn it, this is not what I need to be thinking about. Be here, now, with your friend, I thought.

My pain must have been terribly obvious, because her face suddenly got serious. "What's wrong, Aidan?"

I sighed. "*Hazrah nachti,* okay? Let me share your joy today. Is this your first?"

She perked up. "No. Twice before. First time is very bad, can die. Much easier now."

And with that comment, I realized that the gnolls, true to their appearance, probably have the same unusual reproductive equipment and issues as the spotted hyenas they resemble.

I won't go into it here, but suffice it to say that unless you are a male gnoll who already knows the territory, any lust for a female gnoll is unlikely to end with the results you expect. And I laugh heartily at the academics who speculate that gnoll females are kept separately and never seen, or that male gnolls beget themselves on spotted hyena mothers.

"I never even knew you were a mother! How many?"

"Three each time. Two live now."

And right there is the hard, cold reality of the wild, I thought.

"Have I met them?"

"One. You met Chuka, the female. Males leave the pack when they mature."

"Is she smart?"

"Yes, but not like me. She will not read or write, I think."

"What is she like?"

"Big." She used her arms to pantomime something much larger than her skinny torso. "You saw her, you know." Chuka was huge, and fierce-looking, though a touch shorter than Gryka. She actually had visible muscles, not just fur-covered bones, and given how strong I knew Gryka was, I was frankly terrified of Chuka. "Fast, too. Good legs."

"Is that a problem for gnolls?"

"Slower than lion-men and wolfmen. Maybe never as fast, but we try."

"How is her endurance?" That quizzical look. "How far can she run? Is she just fast on the drop, or can she run all day like you?"

"Maybe not farther, but just as far."

"Good. Be careful of that. There are two kinds of muscle, one for speed and one for endurance. If you switch one for the other, you may gain range but slow down, or go faster but lose range."

She was listening to me very intently.

"Gnolls are red meat, right?"

"Right." She laughed.

"I think that the lighter colored muscles are better for speed and the darker for endurance. Maybe you can find out if that's true with your dead."

"If we can get to them." She grinned. Death for a gnoll usually involves deliberately taking larger and larger chances with bolder and bolder attacks, deep into enemy territory, until she is killed. "We will look for it."

"Anyway, back to your kids. Chuka is smart, but not like you?"

"She is a great hunter, bold, but not too bold. Smart about battle, too. I think she will have many cubs."

"What happened to the male? What was his name?"

"Roko. Good, strong male, not big like Chuka, but so quick! Prey dodges, Roko there step for step. We traded him to the south for Nako. I like Roko better, but he couldn't stay."

"Why not?"

"Females and males both stay, then everyone is family. Mate with who?"

I had to admit that made sense. But..."You could mate outside the pack."

"Mate with male you don't know?" She snorted. "How would you know which to choose? Why not just close eyes, spin in circle, point?" She snorted again. It was the closest I felt I ever got to a taboo...and it wasn't a taboo, really, just disdain for something obviously stupid to her.

"I understand, Gryka." I think.

"Good. You want to understand gnolls? You must understand why that is stupid. If you cannot, ..." A final snort.

"Picking your mate correctly is very important, Gryka. Why is that?"

"Cubs must survive, have own cubs. I think I know best way, what they should be like. I choose father like that."

"If you want more babies, can't you just keep them from killing each other during those first few months?"

"Two teats, not enough milk. Cubs fight from birth, winner always nurses first. Easy to feed three newborns, but they grow so quickly..." She shook her head. "Loser starves unless mother kills one herself, so end with two. Always like this, for everyone."

That hard, cold feral reality again. No wonder gnolls were so strong and tough, and grew so quickly. If the first thing you had to do after you were born was fight your sisters and brothers, probably to the death, you'd be strong and tough and grow up quickly, too.

It made sense, though. Males can mate with multiple females and have more offspring, so they don't care so much who they impregnate. But females can only bear their own offspring, so they invest everything they can in making sure they survive. And unlike most species, which choose mates purely by instinct that may or may not be optimal (like ridiculously long tail feathers, or in our case, huge tits), gnolls apply all their rationality to the process...

...just as they seemed to with everything I asked about. Gnolls are simple, but as far as I can tell, never mystical. No wonder they are better able to hold their own against humans than the other half-humans. Wolfmen seem to spend all their time in clan blood feuds that last for generations and have something to do with ancestor spirits, and lion-men have an exceptionally touchy sense of individual honor which requires them to fight to the death for just about anything any other lion-man says or does—but as the human population expands more and more quickly, gnolls spend more and more time and effort fighting humans for territory, not just other gnolls. They might not be winning, but at least they understand the problem.

Something Gryka said earlier tickled at me. "You said you traded Roko to the south for Nako. What do you mean by 'traded'?"

"Before, just kick males out of pack when grown. Very hard to join new pack as single male. Males in other packs chase off or kill. Had to find females, impress as good mate, also hide from males. Very difficult. Many died."

I nodded. Not impossible, since the other packs would all kick their males out too, but not easy.

"Fights, too. Females see strange male, big, strong, maybe interested. Pack males try to chase away. Females chase pack males, bite ears. Everyone yelling at everyone, fighting."

I laughed out loud. "Arguments for days, I bet."

She nodded. "Never stopped. Now we trade, mostly. Packs meet, all agree no killing, not even *haouka*. Everyone meets male children from other packs, play, talk. Females bargain. 'Roko is fast, very fast. We like your Nyko.' 'Other pack wants Nyko too. You like Taeku?' 'Maybe, but too young yet. Who is mother, father?' Haggle all day, hard work, so important for future!" She grimaced in mock exhaustion. "But fun too. Meet others, not have to think 'Kill, run, or hide?'"

I nodded. What would that be like? To never really be able to meet anyone outside of your pack without having to ask that question? Like most of human history, I realized, but still: so much better this way.

"Males hated at first. Stood with each other, grumbled." I chuckled; I could practically see it myself. "Then males start to think 'New male hunts with us, helps find, track, kill. Don't like one females brought back last time. We come look, talk too.'"

"What happens if no one wants one of your males?" I asked.

"Meetings every six moons, maybe. Go to several, usually some pack wants. If male gets too old, though, no pack wants him, we still kick out."

"So you still have to deal with wandering males."

She grinned. "Not so much, though. Usually smaller, weaker, dumber, or other pack take him already. Other packs know that. Usually dies."

Damn. Every time I started to feel like gnolls were civilized, just like humans with big teeth and claws, Gryka hit me with another blast of hard, cold feral reality. I guess you have to laugh at death when it's right there with you, all the time.

"Do they ever survive, Gryka? Find a pack?"

"Usually, no. But if male survives alone for long time, no pack, chased by everyone, females start thinking 'Maybe tougher than we thought, can help hunt, maybe good mate.' You know Chuko?"

I thought back to the last time I had met their entire pack. "Small, kind of scruffy, missing part of an ear, but looks like you really wouldn't want to fight him?"

"Yes!" she laughed. "Pack to south kicked him out years ago. A runt! We didn't want him, no pack did, his own pack should have killed him, yes? Didn't see for two years, thought dead, *hazrah nachti*. Then he came back, killed Toku, and said 'I hunt with you now.'"

Wait, what? "He just showed up and killed one of your pack, and you said 'Well done! Come with us?'"

"Toku was lazy! Strong, fast, also lazy. Never jump in, hang on, killing bite. Just run, run with pack, always someone else took risk. Also, much bigger than Chuko. Chuko looked half-eaten! Small, fur and bones, missing part of ear, starving. Should have been quick fight, easy."

"What happened?"

"Wore him down. Chuko strikes, slashes, little wounds, bee stings, but Toku can't hit Chuko. Always just past Toku's claws, always moving, moving. Toku wants to grab and bite, can't catch Chuko. Toku loses blood, gets scared, more slashes and grabs, each slower, slower, Chuko slashes him each time. Then Chuko goes under, hamstrings Toku with claws! Toku falls, neck bite, dead. No victory roar, even, Chuko just eats, eats, watching us, eating. So hungry!"

"Fuck!" That was one of the most chillingly brutal stories I'd ever heard, and she sounded like a sports fan recounting last week's rugby match. "And none of you would kill him for that?"

"Maybe before, at start of fight. But no one helped Toku, so pack decided already. Before everyone thought 'Don't like Toku, but rest of pack does, so keep quiet.'" She chuckled. "Chuko is smart. Must have watched us for long time to know that, but we never saw him. Great scout, our best. 'Chuko, how many in pack to north now?' 'Twenty-three, and two *haouka* plan raid tomorrow, maybe next day.' Always comes back."

"So where was he, for those two years?"

"Went north, where it snows sometimes." She shivered. "So cold! Chuko won't talk about it, ever. Always sleeps curled up with someone, even on warm nights. 'Cold for two years, roll over.'" She laughed. "Usually the children, they love him. Plays with little ones all day. So patient!"

"Is he a father? Does he have any of his own?"

"No, not yet, but I think with Chuka someday. She likes Chuko, knows how tough he is. Besides, Chuka almost too big. So strong, but eats too much." She laughed. "Kills extra pig, just for herself!"

My head was buzzing. This was truly astounding. Consciously directed evolution. It was cold, calculating, and so cruel I could barely comprehend it...but absolutely, brutally efficient. Select the traits you believe you need to survive, cull the rest...and if they survive anyway, take them back, no questions, no loyalty to the past, no recrimination for old decisions.

"Gryka. Aren't you afraid, sometimes, that something like what happened to Toku will happen to you? Is there any loyalty at all in your pack? What would happen if you got injured, broke your leg or something?"

She shrugged. "Not lazy, like Toku. Someone attacks me, others come help. Has happened before. Besides, was mother before, now pregnant, so probably again, right? Cubs most important." She grinned. "Broken leg, depends how long. Maybe it sets right, just watch cubs for moon or two, during hunt. Takes longer, though, or pack has to move fast..." She shrugged again. "Happens. *Hazrah nachti.*"

"Is that it, though? Just because you're useful, or might be? Aren't you afraid of being discarded, just like that, the moment you're no longer useful to the pack? How do you live with death so close, right there, every day?"

"Afraid of death?" She grinned the biggest, toothiest, most terrifying grin I'd ever seen, and even before she spoke, my bones knew what she was going to say.

"Afraid of death? WE ARE DEATH!" she roared, raising her hands to strike, claws fully extended. "We eat *meat!* Meat is *dead,* because we *kill it!* Prey dies, we live."

"Humans." She snorted. "Meat is dead, we eat meat, meat is life, we are meat, someday someone eats us. Even gnolls. Afraid of death?" She snorted again. "Afraid of my own shadow, like grass-eaters."

It took me a while to recover from that one. Was it really

that simple? My mind raced around that little circle, over and over. Live meat, dead meat, eat meat, we are meat, go back to step 1.

She continued. "Besides, already have two strong children, maybe third, fourth soon. And if not, rest of pack, other gnolls. All running from death, each generation one step. Death gets me, takes one step. Children and pack and others still one step ahead, death their problem now. Only die once." She laughed.

I smiled ruefully. "I guess you're right. We only die once, then it's over. Why be so scared of something that can only happen once?" I sighed. "I hear you. I understand you. I even believe you. But I can't laugh at death like you do, I'm still scared of it. I guess humans make terrible predators."

She fixed me with a very, very intense stare. *"Then improve."*

My jaw dropped.

Once again I was ready to quit my job, chairmanship be damned. This was like being a fencing master, years in the guild, and some street brawler stabs me right in the face because I'm used to countering the stylized forms of ritual combat and can't deal with a straightforward killing blow.

"Not too much, though. Already tough for gnolls. Need to eat." She grinned at me and loped off, a bit heavily, into the hot, dusty afternoon.

Words

———

"Gryka, I just realized something. You usually speak very simply: short sentences, small words, present tense, dropping articles and conjunctions like you don't understand how to use them, like a second-year language student or Brak the Barbarian. But you seem to understand me just fine even when I use big words and complicated sentences, I've heard you use past and future tense when you absolutely can't get around it, and sometimes you even speak like an educated human. Why is that?"

"Don't like useless words. Like rocks in bird gizzard. Good for bird, no use to me."

And once again, I felt like a half-naked savage talking to a university professor, instead of the other way around.

Problems

———

Since she asked, I showed Gryka how humans used silver-ware to eat: knife, fork, spoon. Surprisingly, she had no trouble at all learning how, and wanted me to show her whether she was doing it correctly: holding her knife and fork properly, switching hands to cut with the knife, and concentrating intensely on what had to be an absolutely useless task to her.

So I asked her. "Gryka, why bother? Your fangs and claws work so much better. I can't even cut a chicken bone with this worthless table knife," I said, brandishing the pretty but annoyingly useless utensil, engraved silver handle and all, "but you can chew the entire drumstick like it was a candy bar. Those giraffe femurs you snap with your jaws? I need a bone saw and several minutes just to cut one in half."

She shrugged. "Passes time."

I whooped. "HA! You're doomed, Gryka! Doomed, doomed, doomed! You, and probably your whole damned pack."

She looked at me with a lopsided but intense look of skepticism. I chuckled grimly.

"That's the forbidden fruit in the Garden of Eden, Gryka. It's the one we ate. Not knowledge. Boredom!" I laughed and shook my head. "Doomed, doomed, doomed."

"Explain." She was suddenly serious.

"Sorry, Gryka. Humans play with ideas like your cubs play with baby animals, except we don't stop when we grow up. Catch it, let it go, chase it again, learning through endless torture and cruelty. If your idea gets torn to pieces and used as a bad example, well, *hazrah nachti*. That's pretty much my life, at the university."

She stared at me intently. I realized this was very important to her, and probably to me as well.

"Anyway, boredom. As I see it, that's the big difference between humans and gnolls. Gnolls don't get bored. If you're hungry, hunt, or eat something you cached. If you're tired, sleep. If times are good and you can find an acceptable mate, fuck him and make some cubs. Always protect your cubs, teach them everything you can, and play with them if there's nothing else to do. If you're dying, go kill the neighbors that piss you off, and if they attack you, kill them." She nodded grimly. "And if that's all taken care of, which it rarely is, find a spot that's safe and a comfortable temperature, and take a nap. Right?"

She nodded, and sighed. "Yes. You remember first thing I

wrote for you?"

That untitled but now-famous document which humans call the Gnoll Credo. I smiled. "How can I forget?"

How, indeed? That's how it all started. All the joy, pain, and blood that came from our long friendship. All because I wanted to figure out what made the gnolls tick—unlike most of the other half-human races or savage human tribes, the slow but steady spread of humans wasn't inexorably displacing and killing them—and I wanted to know why. Why, why, why. And Gryka brought me the Credo, so simple, stark, bloody, beautiful, and most importantly, effective.

"Tear up, throw away. Use what you said instead."

"No!" I protested, dismayed. "You can't be serious. Yours says so much more and sounds so much better."

"Too fancy. Makes us noble. Gnolls not noble."

I had never seen her assailed by self-doubt over anything more than a trivial issue of execution, like "should have checked the interior of the cave before sitting down in it." These ideas were dangerous. Suddenly I realized that involving myself so deeply with Gryka might have terrible consequences after all, no matter how strong she was and how good my intentions were; the thought horrified me.

"No, you're not, you're gnolls, and that's much better. Elves are noble. They're also mostly dead."

She laughed. "Elves taste like chicken. So old, but still so tender! Usually old animal, tough like old boot." She grinned, drooling. "Too much jewelry, though. Sticks in teeth."

And through such unfortunate accidents, I thought, is the course of history altered. I wondered if the elves knew that the slow, tragic decline of their exquisitely beautiful race and culture was mostly due to the fact that their graceful, dignified limbs were absolutely delicious.

"Seriously? Chicken?"

She cocked her head and thought. "Even better. Like chicken, but all white meat. Also, no pee taste." I laughed: chicken has great texture, but it always has that faint sour tang. It's why it tastes better spiced or sauced. Stock up on elf artifacts, kids, they won't be around forever.

"Anyway, let me try to explain the boredom thing, because it's important. Boredom is the corruption, not knowledge. The more you know about hunting, or choosing a mate, or raising cubs, or managing territory, or defending territory, the better off you are, because you do those things better, right?" She nodded. "Even reading and writing lets you get along with humans better, and keep your territory out here that would otherwise be disappearing under houses and farm-steads, without fighting wars all the time. Lots of humans, but still *aregi,* right?"

"Yes. Why I learned."

"So knowledge is good, okay. Now. Boredom corrupts, and absolute boredom corrupts absolutely. The reason is that when you get bored, you start doing things just to fill up the boredom, like learning to use a human knife, fork, and spoon."

She chuckled at that, and I continued. "That isn't the prob-lem by itself, though. The problem, for humans, at least, is that we're competitive. We're competitive at everything. And once we get fixed on a competition, on being the best, it's like we're on a hunt and chasing prey, and we never want to stop until we bring it down. And since there are so many humans, it's very, very unlikely that any one of us is the best at anything." I sighed. "Sorry this isn't coming to a point quickly, Gryka. I'm thinking out loud, here. I just had this insight, and I'm trying to explain it for the first time."

She nodded. "New territory, new animals, hunting is harder."

"Anyway, we get fixated on the competition, on the chase, and we're so intent on winning that we forget why we're competing at all! We forget that the reason was never important, winning won't help us survive, and we only started in the first place because we were *bored!* We forget that it's all a bunch of *nerga. Nerga-nerga-nerga-nerga-nerga.*" I was standing up and shouting now, and people were starting to stare. "We forget about the important things, all that essential stuff you put in the Credo. And *that*," I said, brandishing the useless knife, pointing it straight at her big, blocky forehead, "is why the Credo has to be beautiful. So when you start to get distracted with a whole bunch of *nerga*, there's something bright and shiny to pull your attention back to what's important."

I couldn't read the expression on Gryka's face, but at least I knew I had her full, undivided attention...and that of most of the inn. I was still standing and waving the steak knife around, and I'm sure the innkeeper wanted to kick us out but didn't dare approach the demented, knife-waving maniac, or even worse, the gnoll sitting at his table.

"And you know what's even worse? Maybe gnolls aren't like this, I still don't know. Not as bad as humans, anyway, or you'd already have fallen into the trap." I took a deep breath. "The worst part is that *people can get used to anything*."

"Explain."

"Maybe it's different for gnolls, but for humans, it's like this. If you do something often enough and for long enough, no matter how trivial or painful or useless or self-defeating or just plain stupid, *it changes you*." I ground out the last three words, knowing just how true they were. "It becomes part of you, part of who you are, and you keep doing it, because *that's who you are now*. Do you see?"

She was thinking hard, but didn't seem convinced: I

went on. "We even give it fancy names, depending on how long we've been doing it. Habit, tradition, ritual, culture, religion. You do something often enough, and you get used to doing it that way which just makes you do it more, and you go in little circles, smaller and faster and smaller and faster each time."

"Like bloodlust, in battle. Nothing matters, but the blood. Only stop when you die or kill everything else."

"Exactly! Yes! Except with us, with humans, it happens for anything! No matter how trivial, no matter how painful, no matter how stupid. Anything at all! Hold your fork and knife this way, switch hands to cut. Stupid! Why? Because someone did it, we kept doing it, and now that's just how we do it. There isn't any reason, Gryka. Maybe there never was."

A terrible understanding began to dawn on her face.

"Exactly! Do something often enough, for long enough, and it becomes *its own reason*. Sit in a stuffy building every weekend drinking wine and eating crackers, and believe it's part of your sky-god's body even though cannibalism is bad! Stupid! Why? Because that's just how we do it! Obey the King, even if he's a drooling, inbred idiot and likes fucking little boys with amputations! Stupid! Why? Because that's just how we do it! Sleep alone, no matter how cold it gets! Wear heavy clothes, no matter how hot it gets, because it's wrong to touch or even *see* anyone else's body to whom you're not married! Stupid! Why? Because that's just how we do it! Put grease in your hair, run around poles on May Day, act like you give a shit about opera! Stupid! Stupid! Stupid! Why? Because THAT'S JUST HOW WE DO IT!"

Finally out of breath and out of words, I stabbed the useless little knife into our table and collapsed into my chair. The entire restaurant was staring at me, open-mouthed. Hell, I had been yelling loudly enough that the *entire town* probably heard me.

I didn't care. The void, the black hungry vacuum at the core of my existence that had replaced my soul and allowed me to share the laughter of the gnolls with Gryka, took it all. I was instantly calm.

"And *that* is why boredom is the root of all evil."

Gryka looked stunned, but nodded.

"It's also why I'm so jealous of the gnolls. You haven't forgotten what's important, so you don't get bored like we do...yet. But you are coming to a very, very dangerous time. Deal with humans too much, learn reading and writing, learn too much about us, you can easily start thinking that everything we do is important. It's not. Big, impressive, powerful, destructive, yes, but usually not important. We just got bored."

I blew out a deep breath. "Learn what we do if it is useful to you, or might become useful later. That's fine, that's good, it'll help you survive. But always, always, always! Always in the service of what is important to the gnolls. Never forget that! Please. I don't want to be the man who destroyed gnoll culture."

Gryka grinned. "Gnolls stronger than that. Stronger than you."

"I hope so, Gryka. I really do. Things are changing quickly, you know that. Humans are forcing that change. When everyone lived in little villages like this one, gnolls and wolf-men and lion-men and trolls and ogres and whatever put a check on human population. Now, big cities, growing bigger. When's the last time gnolls, or even ogres, killed anyone in Odene or Sostis, much less made a noticeable dent in the population? Now the gnolls just sneak in to eat corpses out of the graveyard. More and more people, every year. Where are you going to live?"

She nodded. "I think about this."

"Good, because you must. All of you must. Humans will take, and take, and take, and keep taking, just from sheer force of numbers. Individual humans might be helpful or evil, but the end result is the same: more and more of them, less and less of you and everything else. The land can only support so many creatures. You know this better than anyone."

"Yes. All pack hunters know that. Territory too small, not enough prey. Everyone is hungry, always hungry. Get sick, weak, die easy."

"And that's the problem, isn't it? How can you make humans respect your territory? Humans have this idea that they can 'own' land, which is stupid, and that no one else can, which is even stupider. But that's what you're up against. Many of them don't even think you're smart enough to talk, let alone read or write! They think you're just big predators, like lions or wolves, because it's been so long since they've been raided."

"Slackers to south," she snorted. "Hide in forest, never come out."

"It works, though, until the loggers come and cut the forest down. Look, I'm a human, and maybe I'm betraying my own kind by doing this, but I don't think so. I think we need something big and scary to hunt us, so we don't keep forgetting what's important. But the mass of humans don't respect a single predator, no matter how huge or scary. March everyone in Sostis out of the gates, even naked and unarmed, and they could kill an entire baluchithere just by smothering it under their bodies. Thousands would die, but we've got thousands. Maybe even a hundred thousand, just in and near Sostis."

She nodded. "Like swarm of bees. Smother wasp. Hundreds die, but hive saved."

"Humans will tell you a lot of self-serving crap. High-minded advice, noble promises. We'll lie to you all day if we think it'll fool you into giving us something, and we won't feel guilty, even a bit, because you're not human. Do this, do that, learn this, come to our schools, sign this treaty giving up part of your territory, it's only fair, oh, you did it wrong, sorry, if you would just act civilized we'd give you some rights, try again."

Deep breath. "And it's all bullshit, Gryka. It's all bullshit. At the end of the day, it's about *strength*." I slapped the table for emphasis. "It's about who can take what, and who can hold on to it once they take it. If you want to survive, you'll have to be strong enough to hold your territory against humans. First, they send settlers. Kill too many, they send a detachment, maybe with knights. You've seen this, right?"

She nodded. "Long ago. I was barely adult. Handful of archers, maybe, farmers with pikes. Easy kills for gnolls." She snorted. "Knights easy too, once archers dead. Cripple horse, knight useless."

"Someday, though, they'll send an entire army! You can probably kill ten soldiers for every gnoll that dies, but the Duke of Sostis alone has an army of ten thousand. Have you ever seen ten thousand people, Gryka? Even one thousand?"

Gryka was concentrating, hard. "Not ten thousand, but I imagine. Big lake, full of humans."

"Humans with swords, Gryka. Swords, shields, pikes, halberds, lances. Cavalry. A whole line of armored knights, not just one or two. And hundreds of archers. Battle starts, arrows fall like rain. Makes you want to go hide in the forest and not come out, doesn't it?"

She nodded. "Stay out of trouble. Don't like big battles. Too many swords and arrows, too easy to die of bad luck."

"But if you stand up and say 'No, this land is ours, this is our territory, it belongs to the gnolls,' that army will be sent after you, your pack, and every other pack that happens to be in the way. Do you understand?"

After a long pause, she nodded.

"There is one exception. The king will only send his army if he thinks he can win—and that the cost of winning is worth it for what he will get. You don't need ten thousand to his ten thousand. You just have to make him believe that it will cost him too much to win. Helps if he's fighting someone else at the time, too."

I laughed and shook my head. "Diplomacy, Gryka. Humans write entire books about it, devote their entire lives to it. Some people, that's all they do; the king pays them to gauge strength, find weakness, help negotiate, make decisions. I'm not a diplomat, I'm a professor, but even I can tell that you can't do it the way we do, not without giving up everything that's good about being gnolls, not without turning into big, furry, ugly people."

She snorted. "Wearing shirts and trousers, pretending to like what king likes. No good."

"So what the hell do the gnolls do, Gryka? How can they, how can you become something with enough power, that commands enough respect, to keep anything at all of your own? How can you stand against the endless, teeming, grow-ing, breeding tide of humans without either being slaughtered or changing into something just like us?"

"I don't know, Aidan. But I know one thing, now."

Her eyes were hard, but they glittered.

"I will never be bored. Never. This problem, it is here." She tapped her head. "Here for long time, but in distance. Always running. Sometimes stotting, like springbok." I laughed: that was vivid. "More important now, though. Gnolls do not live long, like humans."

I knew that, but I had always avoided facing the nearly

inevitable consequence: Gryka would die well before I did. I knew she was not young, but I didn't know how old; I could have asked her, and I was sure she'd have told me, but I wasn't sure I wanted to know the answer.

"Hunt will be difficult, take long time. Generations. Gnolls can do that."

I raised my eyebrow, which Gryka took as disbelief. "Ha! You think gnolls are always this strong? Can always run so fast, for so long? Always smart enough to read and write, just never did?"

"Actually, yes, I guess I did. But I never thought about it much."

She snorted. "You think we choose mates by lining up males, spinning rock?" I whooped. "For nice ears, soft coat, spots in right place?" She snorted again. "I tell story."

That sat me back. Gryka had never told me a story, ever. Asked questions, answered my questions, argued, but I had never once heard her say "Once upon a time..."

She fixed me with her stare. That was another thing... Gryka, like every gnoll I had met, always looked directly at me when she spoke. Always. And when it wasn't practical— talking while walking or running—she rarely spoke, constantly scanning her surroundings for potential threats or prey. I didn't know whether it was a dominance tactic, sign of courtesy, or just how they were; I made up my mind to ask, later.

"Many generations ago. No one knows number, we didn't count then. Many generations ago, a female was...different. Before then, always the same. Males bigger than females, males fight, biggest male picks females, fucks them, female bears cubs, like lions or zebras. We were smaller then, not as smart. Like any other predator. Same for long time.

"But then, a female was...different. Was female cub, but looked like male. Cock, balls. You see mine, ever?" She pushed her chair back as if to stand up.

Oh, no. "Not here, Gryka. I'll never eat here again, and it's the only inn in town. I'm surprised they haven't kicked us out already, after my rant earlier."

"You were waving knife, yelling like gnoll in battle. All frozen in place, like fawns!" She laughed and pulled her chair forward again. I grinned.

So I was right. Gnolls were exactly like spotted hyenas, and it was a mutation, probably dominant, and I knew (or thought I knew) how this story would go, but I really wanted to hear her tell it.

"New female grows up as male, takes male place in pack, starts to fight. Smells wrong, though. Males and females both confused. But new female is big like males, good hunter, good fighter, strong. Finally fights male first-eater, wins. New first-eater usually chases old first-eater out of pack, but new female is different.

"New female says to pack 'I eat first, and I am female. I choose mates now.' Pack confused, but none will fight her. Males confused, but horny."

I laughed, and Gryka laughed with me. "Males all the same, everywhere, every species. Promise sex, brains dribble out ears." Damn it, I was even starting to talk like her, simple tenses, dropping articles. Better kick that habit, I thought. Can't publish papers that sound like they were written by Brak the Barbarian, no matter how complete and closely reasoned.

"New female was smart. Before, males kill cubs of other males, female stops nursing, can mate again. Now she picks three favorite males, says 'I mate with all three of you. Cubs may be yours, yes?'

"Three other males say 'This is wrong. Males must choose. Maybe one of us cannot fight you alone, but all three can. We will bite you and rape you.'

"New female laughs. 'How? Even if you hold me with your jaws, where will you put your cock? Mine is as big as yours. You can kill me, but you cannot rape me. And I will kill one of you before I die, maybe two, maybe all three.' Males back down.

"New female mates. Males confused. What goes where? Everyone horny, try different things, finally solve problem.

"New female grows large with cubs. Three males help defend her, feed her, could be theirs, yes? Birth terrible, painful, cock splits open, new female almost dies, but female cub is like her, cock and balls, big, aggressive. Mates again, birth much easier, another new female. Cubs grow up, breed true.

"Young males, driven out of other packs, join pack with new females. Any male too low to mate thinks 'Maybe chance over there,' comes. And new females kill many old males too." She grinned fiercely. "Everything changed."

Wow.

"Gryka, how do you know that story?"

"Got from mothers. Feels right, though."

"It's not exactly the same now, though, is it? Females don't still mate with many males at once, do they?"

"Males trained now. No need." I chuckled at that. "Still happens sometimes, if female can't decide, or just for fun. Need some competition, or males get too docile. Cock and balls shrink, don't want to hunt, sit around, talk about feelings."

I choked on my beer, spraying a fine mist all over our table, Gryka, and the blessedly empty table next to us. As I collapsed in helpless laughter, she reached across the table and flicked my ear, hard, drawing blood with her claw. "Ow!"

"Hate beer. Smells like piss." She scowled, but her eyes twinkled as she wiped herself down with a table napkin. She was human enough to feel pleased about telling a good joke, even by accident.

Once she finished cleaning up, I prompted her: "You were talking about long projects. Generations."

"Still going there. Long way, takes time." She paused, and drank a swallow of water. Gnolls are adapted to dry climates, and don't need to drink much; we had been here quite a while. But this was fascinating, and I had no intention of interrupting. "Choosing mates. Males want all the females, all the cubs they can sire. Females carry, nurse, some will survive, no problem, let females worry. Females want every one of their cubs to survive. Each one important, can't just fuck again, make more like male can."

I nodded. How much did the gnolls understand about natural selection? I was about to find out.

"So choosing right mate is everything for female, because of cubs. Nothing is more important to her. Important for rest of pack, too. Strong pack better for everyone. Better hunting, easier life. Even if cub isn't yours, better for you if smart, strong, good hunter."

Conversing with Gryka was getting me out of the human habit of responding to everything anyone said, whether I had anything to say or not. I waited, watching her.

She continued. "Cubs usually grow up like mother, father, yes? Maybe also grandmothers, grandfathers. But what is best for cub, for pack? 'Big, strong.' Too big, eat too much, always hungry. 'Fast, fast.' Not tough enough, break legs, arms, teeth. Females talk, think, talk more. Cubs not always like parents anyway, but we try."

Amazing. Women sitting in their sewing circle, talking about survival characteristics, deciding what's most important for their future and the pack, choosing mates based on their decisions. Except the 'sewing circle' probably meets around a zebra carcass they've just killed, eviscerated, and eaten, and its members are even bigger and fiercer than the males.

"So many questions! Older male has survived long time, we know well. But not too old, or can't help with cubs. And if children grow up well, older male is dead, no more cubs from him. But younger male, not sure yet. Great hunter, fierce warrior, maybe just lucky? Quiet, or stupid?" She laughed. "Talk for hours."

I could see it, I really could. "But that's not a generational project, that's just this generation, now. What are you doing that takes longer?"

"Long time ago, decided was important for gnolls to be bigger, stronger. Needed big packs to kill big prey, defend kills against lion-men. Too many died on hunts, packs too big, too many fights. Also, hard to use human, elf weapons, gnolls too short. Much easier now." She grinned. "Before, just spears, slings. Claws, teeth were better. Then bows, we could make, use. Then swords! Better than claws!" Her eyes gleamed.

"Wait a minute. So you're saying you bred yourselves bigger and stronger *just so you could use human weapons?*"

"Already getting bigger for big prey, though, so almost done already. Then, saw that when gnolls taller than humans, humans get scared, fight badly. Sometimes run, drop weapons!" She laughed. "Scared other gnolls, too."

Gryka was right. Even though they were usually skinny, the fact that gnolls towered over humans made them absolutely nightmarish. I tried to imagine a short gnoll...same teeth, same claws, but chest height...no. To be avoided, yes, but not terrifying.

"So then gnolls say 'Tall more important than big. Also, getting too big, eating too much meat.' All skinny now. Used to be shorter, thicker, like hyena. Hard to keep strength when so skinny, had to fight differently. But we run much faster now."

If I stopped to think too much about the implications, my brain was going to explode...so I just ran with it. "Is there a gnoll fighting technique?"

She snorted. "Should children flail like cubs? We train. Each pack different, but similar. Fighting is fighting."

"Wait...I just thought of something. You talk like all the gnolls decided to breed for size, strength, height at once—but you run in packs, you defend your territory fiercely, you rarely talk to those in other packs...are you talking about just your pack, or all the gnolls? And if everyone, how do you get the word out to other packs that will probably kill you if they can?"

"Probably one pack started. But males leave pack when grown, so news travels. Slowly, but changes take many generations. Now packs meet to trade males, news travels much faster. Also, packs decide differently. Good decisions, pack kills others, more territory. Bad decisions, pack gets killed, loses territory. Tall, skinny, fast was good decision." She grinned. "Almost all gnolls like us now."

Damn. "How many generations did this take, Gryka?"

"No one knows. Didn't count, back then."

"For how long have you counted?"

She grinned. "Gnoll secret. More generations than your fingers and toes."

And that is a long, long time, even in gnoll generations, and there was the answer to my question.

Like most answers, though, it just suggested more

questions. I thought for a while, in silence, until the big one took shape.

"If you're consciously directing your own evolution, then there have to be a lot of you that don't get killed in hunts or battle, but still don't make the cut. Maybe someone is a great hunter, quick, strong, tough, but too short. What do you do with them, and who decides? Why would they stay around? What's in it for them? Why shouldn't they try to sabotage things, get a chance?"

Gryka laughed. "Too many questions! Ask one."

"Someone runs with the pack, hunts, survives, but you know the higher-ranking females will never let her mate. Or, you know a male will never be chosen as a mate. What do you do?"

"For males, always hope. Could happen someday, yes?" She grinned. (Women are more cruel than men. This is true with any animal. Never doubt it.) "For females, if no good, we kill them, eat."

My face must have shown my shock, because Gryka said "No pain. Kill quick, while sleeping, mostly."

I was still dumbfounded. This was far worse, more brutal than I had imagined.

"What else?" she asked me. "Live entire life, watching others make cubs, hating rest of pack for stopping you? And for rest of us, plots, revenge, suspicion, hatred, fighting, pack dies. No good. Better they die quickly. Otherwise, die slowly, take others with them."

It had its own cruel logic. And despite my instinctive horror and revulsion, I couldn't honestly figure out a way to convince her otherwise. Human society hasn't solved the problem for millennia, so we just bumble on, filling up the land until we die of famine or start another cruel, bloody war. I doubt the total suffering is any less, and I have an unsettling suspicion that the gnolls' way is actually less cruel in the long run—they kill their own quickly and painlessly, and even feed the pack by it, instead of pretending conflict doesn't exist until it explodes into riots, wars, revolutions, and at the individual level, random violence. Get drunk, break things and people, kill regret with drink, repeat.

"So what keeps the highest-ranked female from just killing all the other females, and having all the children?"

"Not enough cubs. Pregnant, nursing, three years maybe, only two cubs, some die anyway. Also, hard to lead pack if always pregnant, nursing, training children. Also, raids from other packs."

"What?"

"When other packs raid, they try to kill females, so no more cubs. High rank, if they can. Killing males no problem, don't need so many. You see?"

Oh. "So if there aren't enough females, and one or two get killed..."

"No more cubs, pack dies."

"Then, could those males ever kidnap females from other packs?"

"How? If they can't kill them, how kidnap them? No females because of losing fights, right?"

"Hmmm...I guess you're right. Would they kidnap female cubs, maybe? Raise them, mate with them when they mature?"

She hooted and whooped with laughter, taking quite a while to calm down. I didn't understand...it didn't seem funny to me at all.

"No, seriously, Gryka. Why not? Seems like it could happen."

"Never." She shook her head. "New females, never. Rape impossible, remember? Also, cock and balls make us too aggressive. Run pack anyway." She smirked.

"Why humans have big wars, maybe," she said. "Humans think 'We are peaceful, smell flowers, grease hair, go to opera, never hungry, all find mates, everyone happy.' War is different, stupid, wrong, should not happen, yes?"

I nodded. That was basically the popular opinion, substituting your own choice of recreation for "grease hair, go to opera."

"Gnolls kill and eat problems. Cub misshapen, sickly, stupid? Kill and eat. Too badly injured, can't recover, always crippled? Kill and eat. No one wants male? Kill and eat."

"I thought you just led them on forever."

"Mostly. Sometimes too useless. Anyway, gnolls kill and eat problems fast. Humans go other way around. Problems mate, have little cub problems, grow into adult problems, big, dangerous. And so many! Gnoll problems hard enough, how to survive in future with crazy humans." She winced. "Makes head hurt."

Given that I worked for the University, a large institution full of very smart people whose stated purpose is to solve human problems, and that we can't even agree on what those problems are, let alone how to solve any of them—I couldn't find a way to disagree with her.

We both had a lot of problems to think about that night.

Bridge

—

"Aidan. What do your cock and balls look like?"

I thought I was used to Gryka's random questions, but that one got me. "Like a cock and balls. Why?"

"Saw other human's once or twice, long way away, wondering if all the same. Show me."

Well, we knew each other well enough by this point, so why not? But then I chuckled. "I'll show you mine if you show me yours."

That got me a quizzical expression. "Yes, but what's funny?"

"Old human joke," I said, unbuttoning my trousers. "Little kids, curious, boys about girls, girls about boys, each other."

Gryka took a moment to catch on. "Yes. Even baby humans wear clothes. Why?"

"For babies, it's a diaper, so they don't piss or shit on the floor. Stays in the diaper."

She laughed. "Baby humans. So helpless! Gnoll cubs already smart enough not to shit in tunnels, on mother."

"Humans take much longer to grow up, you know that. Also we don't have to kill our brother or sister right after we're born."

She grinned. "Why so shy, human?" I realized I had been talking to her with my trousers around my ankles. Well, I had plenty to show, I thought, nothing to be ashamed of downstairs—but it still felt strange, undressing in front of a gnoll. Oh, hell with it, I thought. Stop being a prude. I dropped the underwear and unbuttoned my shirt, which was hanging over everything.

Gryka stepped over and examined it critically. "Does it always hang downward like that?"

"More or less. Depends on how hot it is and whether I'm thinking about sex."

"Big, too. No wonder humans always cover it. Bouncing around like canteen on belt when you run."

"Not always that big, I'm lucky," I corrected her: she laughed. "And that may have been why, a long time ago, but women cover theirs too. Nothing to bounce." I grinned. "Hey, no fair, where's yours?"

She shrugged, and rotated the leather belt that held her small loincloth—as well as her well-used belt knife, minimal fire-starting tools, a tiny sharpening stone for both the knife and her claws, and a small, carefully sealed pouch that contained written material if she had any with her. (Any contract with gnolls always came back well-folded.) I was jealous: Gryka was totally self-sufficient anywhere with less *nerga* than was usually in my pockets, and didn't really need any of it—a knife and fire were luxuries to her, like a hot bath and maid service were to me.

I knew from what Gryka had said before that female gnolls, like female hyenas, were extremely masculinized, and had basically the same equipment as the males—including a long, tubular clitoris that they even pissed through, and "balls" that were just fatty pouches, but which sure looked real. It was still unsettling, though, to see them on a female who was still lactating, and more than a bit intimidating that she was hung at least as well as I was. Like most animals, her "cock" was in a pouch that faced upward, so it didn't bounce or flap around when she ran, and the "balls" were very tight to her body.

"Gryka, why do gnolls bother with loincloths? Your junk doesn't bounce around like ours. Don't tell me gnolls are modest?"

She made a sour face. "Think, Aidan. Gnolls always running, on hunt. Bushes, branches, sometimes thorns."

Ow. "That's why you don't make them for cubs or little children, right? Not hunting yet?"

She nodded. "Also, balls not dropped yet, hurts less. Grow too fast anyway, have to make new one every moon. We wait until they ask."

Made sense to me. "How old when they usually ask? Does it mean anything?"

"Yes. Means they want to be adult, not child."

"What does that mean?"

She had to stop and think about that. "Means they still might be small, weak, but ready for pack to trust with important things. Children small, sneaky, very fast sometimes. Can be useful."

"Do you ever refuse when someone asks to wear one?"

"No, never. But you say 'I am adult now,' you are...wait, missing word." Her brow wrinkled. "For child, do stupid thing, just silly child. We notice, but still...doesn't matter so much, yet."

"Responsibility? Is that the word?"

"Yes!" Her eyes lit up. "Say 'I am adult now,' do stupid thing, then you are stupid, lose pack trust. Do smart thing, then you are smart, gain pack trust. Responsibility."

I had to admit that it made sense. Some human kids grow up quickly, some take much longer, but we pretend they're all the same even though some are shaving at twelve and some are still eating cake frosting out of the bowl. "So do gnolls grow up all at once? 'Here's your belt and loincloth, son, no more food for you?'"

Gryka laughed. "No, then who would want one? Still different life, though. Hunt with children, don't expect to eat, just teach children. Child says 'Adult now, hunt with you,' we expect to eat. Maybe too small to kill, but can still track, chase."

I nodded. "But what happens if someone grows up—I mean physically, balls drop, whatever—but refuses to say 'I am adult now'?"

She laughed. "Lots of scratches on cock, balls. Also, refuse too long, we kill and eat."

And there it was again—that brutally efficient feral ethic which always stunned me with its casual violence, but that I couldn't find a way to argue with. "Does that ever actually happen?"

"Haven't seen it. Children don't get enough meat for grown adult, mother would stop feeding slacker anyway." She grinned. "And hunting is fun, best thing ever! Gnoll doesn't want to hunt?" She snorted. "Like fish saying 'Don't like water.' Soon, dead fish."

I whooped with laughter, which died down into a wistful chuckle. Gryka's life was violent, dangerous, and would be short by human standards even if she lived to her full potential lifespan—but it was, as far as I could tell, completely free of self-doubt, as it was for the other gnolls I had spoken with. *Hazrah nachti*, I thought. I wished humans could find that center, and realized I'd settle for finding it myself, because even that was more than most of us ever accomplished in our lifetimes.

I also realized my trousers and underwear were still around my ankles, and I should ask a couple more questions as long as we were both standing there checking out each other's junk. "Gryka, I've wondered about this for a while. Hyenas, and most social quadrupeds, spend a lot of time sniffing and licking each others' genitals. I know it's social signaling and has to do with dominance and submission and all that. But gnolls stand upright, so it's much harder to do that all the time...and now that you're wearing those loincloths, it's got to be harder to smell, and you can't see when someone's cock comes out. Does any of that still happen, ever?"

She nodded. "Much less often, now. Hyenas are smart, but gnolls much smarter. Don't need to sniff, lick always to know who's who. We remember."

"So why does it still happen at all?"

"Need to remind others, sometimes. Get frisky, forget place." And she grinned a huge, completely symmetrical, and utterly terrifying grin. "Male gets uppity at kill, throws elbow. LICK MY BALLS!" she roared.

I swear my hair parted in the middle and my cock shrank an inch, and she was so fiercely commanding that I almost bent down and did it, right there, and she saw me start and threw her head back and howled with helpless laughter, and as the sudden tension slowly drained from my body I started laughing, too, because my trousers and underwear were still sitting there around my ankles and her loincloth was still sitting over her hip and I finally let go and howled along with Gryka, imagining all the poor bastards over the years who had to kneel before her and actually do it.

Still chuckling, she readjusted her belt and loincloth as I pulled my underwear and trousers back up and messed with buttons and drawstrings. I burst out laughing again.

Gryka looked at me inquiringly. "Another human joke?"

"Standing in room with female, putting on clothes, usually means we just had sex."

She smiled, a sad, wistful smile. "You're not a gnoll, Aidan. Smell wrong, cock wrong shape, can't make cubs."

"Same here, my cock isn't interested. I love you, you know that, but...*kazhda,* right?"

"*Kazhda.* Besides, mating over quick. We have more fun, yes?" She grinned, and cuffed me on the shoulder—the one with the scars.

"Yes. Yes, we do. But I'd still give it all up to be a gnoll with you, you know that."

We hugged for a long moment, a bridge spanning two very, very different worlds. Usually the bridge we build is more beautiful than the two places it joins and this was a beautiful bridge indeed, new and wide and lit up like the night sky, and maybe it would even outlast the two of us—but I still would have burned it in an instant if I could just have crossed it first.

Future

———

Twilight had finally faded to night, and since the heat of the day still lingered inside my house, we were standing outside on the small balcony, watching the stars.

"Gryka," I asked, "what do gnolls think about the future?"
She looked at me, puzzled.
Well, it was a strange question. "What I mean is, you don't seem to believe in gods or demons..."
"Idiots to north. Draw pictures on weapons, on self, think it matters." She snorted pungently. "Draw eye on rock, rock cannot see. Even children know that."

"Right. But the reason they, and lots of humans, worship gods is because they think gods control their future."

"Don't think so. Priests say 'Pray to god, god helps you, don't pray, god hurts you.' Never seen it." She paused. "People think too much. Gnolls look at clouds, see weather. Humans look at clouds, see animals, monsters." She shrugged. "Same with gods. Gnoll gored on hunt, killed by *haouka,* should have been faster or more careful, *hazrah nachti.* Humans lose battle, starve because of no rain, think gods are angry because of something they did."

That short little speech brought about six different questions to my mind—I hoped I would remember some of them. "But I've seen you talk about constellations."

Another puzzled look. "Don't know word."

"Seeing pictures in the stars."

She laughed. "Yes. Helps us find direction, time of night, season. Don't think pictures mean anything, though, like humans. Just easier to remember, teach children."

I thought about astrology and alchemy, and laughed with her. "Maybe humans do think too much. Always trying to find reasons for everything, even when there isn't one, just good or bad luck."

"Always a reason, Aidan. Always."

I looked up at her, surprised.

"Usually doesn't matter, though, just call it luck. Herd scatters left, not right. Who understands reasons of wildebeest, of impala?"

"So you believe that other animals think, too, like gnolls and humans?"

"Of course! Stupider, though." She laughed. "Zebras are mean, but dumb. Think 'I'll hide in herd, gnolls confused by stripes, kill someone else.' Gnolls don't care, all zebras taste the same."

I chuckled. "Probably works for that zebra, though. That's why they all have confusing stripes. Any zebra who didn't would be too easy for gnolls to keep track of."

Gryka laughed. "Yes! Brown zebra! So easy to see, single out, kill!"

"See?" I grinned. "Maybe stupid for zebras in general, not so stupid for each individual zebra."

She concentrated hard for a moment. "Impala, same. Jump around like fleas when we chase them. Stupid for impalas, but maybe smart for each impala. Gnolls lose it in herd, single out another."

"Right. Any impala that didn't jump around with everyone else would be easier for gnolls to eat."

She smiled. "This is why I talk with you, Aidan. Learn new things. Why all herd animals do same thing, even stupid things. Don't follow herd, get singled out, eaten, even if smarter."

I sighed. "Same with all animals, even humans. Except humans are our own predators. Look too different, act too differently, kings or priests or nobles or belligerent drunks shun you or even kill you for it." I paused. "That's why I work at the University. We're expected to look and act differently, play with ideas, so long as we don't try to convince the rest of the world to take them seriously. If I started traveling like a preacher, speaking about living without kings or God or gods, I'd be jailed or killed. Why are gnolls different, Gryka?"

"We're not, Aidan. We kill and eat each other, remember?"

"It's not the same, though...you kill cripples and the weak, true. But if a male is different, you just kick him out—and you'll take him back if he survives anyway. Like Chuko, right?" She nodded. "Or like you, even. You're reading, writing, spending all this time with me, talking about strange new ideas—but your pack doesn't kill you for it."

"Still good hunter," she said. "Strong, fast, pack trusts me. Others think 'Strange, don't understand sometimes, but still good gnoll.' My children are strong, too. Most important thing."

"I wish humans were that clear-headed. But what can I do about it when the herd is all muddle-headed and they will kill me for being too different?"

"Don't know. Maybe find others, start new herd."

And *that*, I thought to myself, is the history of every religious and political heresy, usually ending in torture and death for everyone involved.

"Humans." She shook her head, puzzled. "So strange. Sometimes act like predators, sometimes like prey. Don't understand at all."

I didn't either, until much later—so I just left it there and went back to my original question. "Gryka, I've always been a bit puzzled by *hazrah nachti*. Terrible things happen, your packmate dies, everyone is sad, maybe cries some, but you all seem to accept it very quickly, as though it was fated to happen and there's nothing you can do. But gnolls work so hard to survive, fighting death every day with all their strength, and you said earlier that there's always a reason for everything. So what do you think about the future, anyway? How can you work so hard to change the future, yet accept it so quickly when it comes?"

She thought about that for a long moment, and spoke slowly. "Future just in head. Hasn't happened yet. Talk about 'future,' really saying 'What I think future will be.'" A pause. "So future always changing. Think 'Herd by mountains tomorrow, hunt there, fill stomach,' go there, no herd. Future changes. Think 'Mate with big male, have big children,' child is skinny, fast, like grandmother. Future changes."

Another pause. "Why gnolls laugh at humans. 'If this, then

if that, then if, if, if.' *Nerga, nerga, nerga.* Too many 'ifs'. Meanwhile, empty stomach." She laughed, and I laughed with her, recalling how many times I had worked late into the night and forgotten to eat.

"Maybe that's why it's so simple for gnolls," I said. "You're still hunters. Hunting is dangerous, you can get hurt or die. But if you don't hunt, you starve, definitely die. No choice, really."

She nodded, and grinned. "Yes. Big hunt tomorrow morning, too. Must return to pack now, sharpen claws, mind. Then sleep." She hugged me, easily vaulted the railing, dropped almost silently to the street ten feet below, and loped off into the night.

Milk

—

Ever since last year's long conversation about how gnolls could hold their own against humans, I had been thinking about what sort of technology, if any, they might be able to use. As usual, things didn't go quite like I expected.

One night I intended to ask Gryka about milk. "I know gnolls would never be interested in agriculture, even if they could eat plants..."

"Up and down same field all day, sitting on plow, watching ass end of ox. Cannot eat ox, must make ox do tricks. Go here, turn, now go there. *Worst circus ever.*" She snorted, and I laughed. "Die of boredom, three days. Dirt is not hair, why comb it? Plants still grow."

"But not the plants you want."

"Meat eats plants for us. We eat meat."

"What do gnolls know about plants?"

"Enough. What plants prey likes, where they are. Waiting-root. Poison dirt."

"Poison dirt? Why would you eat dirt, let alone poisonous dirt?"

She chuckled. "Dirt not poison. Eat dirt with poison. Hurts less."

"Just any dirt?"

"No, special kind of clay." Probably bentonite. Considering their cast-iron stomachs can digest carrion and bones, I was afraid to ask what was strong enough to be poisonous to a gnoll.

Suddenly I realized that my milk herd idea was stupid. Gnolls sucking milk out of a cow? I couldn't take the thought seriously with those wicked teeth and sharp claws right there in front of me. The cows would flee in terror anyway.

But plants...gnolls didn't pay much attention to plants. Maybe they should. "Gryka, I just had an idea. Plants are for your prey to eat, right. But what if you grew plants, not for you, but for your prey? Humans do that sometimes. We grow corn or hay, and feed it to cows. Mostly further north, so they won't die in the winter, when the grass is under the snow and doesn't grow." Gnolls might not know that, I thought, since they didn't live anywhere it snowed regularly.

"Grow plants for prey?" She scowled. "Soon, groom prey, pull out ticks? Sing to sleep?" She snorted.

I laughed. "No, not like humans, with ox and plow. You're right, worst circus ever. But maybe if there are plants your prey likes to eat, help scatter their seed, pull up other plants."

Gryka looked stunned, and she remained silent for a long moment. "Humans. So strange." Another long pause. "Gnolls very good at thinking 'How?', but not so good at thinking 'If...' Humans always thinking 'If, if, if...'" She paused. "We laugh. If zebras have wings, river flows uphill, sun rises in west, what if? So stupid!" She laughed. "But then you say 'Why not sow plants for prey to eat, more prey live?' Gnolls never think of that. Only humans think backwards, upside down, say 'What if?' Stupid, stupid, stupid, but then..."

She sighed. "Like being told 'See little green river rocks? Is meat, delicious!' Laugh, but see other gnoll eating them, chewing, swallowing, 'Won't hunt today, not hungry, stay with cubs.'"

"I think that's why the gnolls are so tough, though," I said. "Always asking 'How?', always focused on your surroundings and your own survival. Ask 'What if...?' too much, stop paying attention to the world around you, and a *haouka* from the neighboring pack sneaks up and bites your head off."

She nodded. "Could be. Humans say 'daydreaming,' right? Gnolls never daydream. Always looking for threats or prey, always."

"Do gnolls dream, Gryka?"

"Yes. All animals dream. Hunt, battle, mating." She grinned.

An idea nagged at me. "I wonder...Gryka, is it possible for gnolls to learn how to think 'What if...?' To practice it, train for it, like you train your children to fight? Not like humans, daydreaming, lost in thought, but with focus and purpose, like gnolls?"

She said nothing, listening intently.

But how would a gnoll do that? Think like a scientist, I told myself, and I grinned. "I think I know how. Think of something that you want but can't get, then ask 'How?' Like my idea of sowing plants for prey to eat. You say 'Zebras, antelope are tasty. Wish there were more of them. How?'"

She shrugged. "Need more territory."

"No. Zebra lives. How?"

"Eats grass, maybe flowers, little bushes."

"But there is a lot more than grass in your territory. Trees, bushes, vines, flowers, many different kinds. Zebras don't eat all of them. What don't zebras eat?"

Her face lit up. "Thornbush! Nothing eats thornbush, maybe goats sometimes. So much of it. More every year."

"So if there were more grass and less thornbush, there could be more zebras and antelope, right? More for zebras and antelope to eat?"

She grinned. "Also, easier to find pigs. Run into thornbush, can't catch."

"So. Less thornbush, more zebras, pigs to eat. How?"

A long pause. "Prickly, tough, hard to cut. Gnolls know how to hunt, kill animals, but not how to hunt, kill plants." At that, we both laughed.

I pounced. "See? That's 'What if...?' It's not magic. Just say 'I want this,' and keep asking 'How?', step by step. If you only see the start and the end, of course it seems like a magic trick, but it isn't."

"Still difficult, though. New territory, new prey. Don't know what is dangerous, what is good to eat, where prey eats, dens."

"But you can do it, though. Gnolls can do it. You've just never had to, before."

She nodded. "Everything changing now, so fast! Humans." She shook her head. "Each one so slow, weak, mostly stupid. Then steel! Swords! Cities! Humans everywhere!" She took a deep breath, blew it out. "We know gnolls must change too, but how? So little time."

"I don't know, either, Gryka. But you're doing the right things. Learning to read and write, learning to enter into contracts with humans, learning to think about a future that might be different from the present. I think being smart is much more important for the gnolls now than being tall and scary. That works on settlers, villagers, even a detachment with a knight or two—but it won't frighten off an entire army. Professional military men might be scared, but they'll fight anyway."

She nodded. "We know this. Choosing mates for brains, now, much more than before. Like Nako. Not so big, not best hunter, but mind so quick! Quicker than me. Quiet, though. Strange."

She paused, and shook her head. "But if all gnolls are like Nako, what are gnolls?"

I didn't know, either.

But then I did. "Alive," I said.

She gave me one of her totally inscrutable looks, and then burst into laughter. "Yes! You think like gnoll now!" She kept chuckling. "Also, two parents. Nako's cubs not exactly like Nako. Maybe more like me."

"Wait, you mated with Nako?" My jaw dropped, and I realized I had forgotten to ask who the father was, back when she first told me she was pregnant. "I don't believe it." Picture a skinny teenage chess prodigy with an Amazon warrior queen.

"Brains most important now, yes? Nako hears everything, remembers everything. So smart! Maybe children get my body, his brains. Also, Nako good at mating. Was pregnant right away, but told him 'Not sure, better try again,' next few nights." She grinned a huge, lopsided grin and hung her tongue out, panting. "Lasted so long! Nice big cock, too."

I laughed: score one for the nerds. Good for you, Nako. "Do gnolls ever mate just for fun, like humans?"

"Almost never. Mate with male, cubs come, pack must

help. Never mate without pack knowing first, or big problems. Once pregnant, don't want to mate again, after first few days anyway." She grinned hugely again.

"*Almost* never?" I asked, with my own lopsided grin.

"Sometimes mate while pregnant, out of estrus, but rare. No fun for female. Favor to male, like grooming, licking." She shrugged. "Both know it means nothing. We can all smell estrus, whose cubs are whose."

"I wish humans could do that, because it would solve so many of our problems." I sighed. "So who decides who can mate, get pregnant?"

"Females above you. You want to mate, make cubs, must ask females above you."

"Why would they ever say 'yes'? Why not just have them all themselves?"

Gryka laughed. "Already told you! Who wants to be pregnant or nursing all the time? Also, not enough cubs. Life is short, so many of us die, cubs, children, adults. Need cubs or pack dies. Also, maybe low-rank females disobey, make cubs anyway. No one wants big fight, maybe killing. Remember, small pack, everyone talking, all the time. Everyone knows everything."

I could just imagine.

We sat for a while in companionable silence. With Gryka, silence was fine.

"Listen, Gryka, I have to leave tomorrow, okay? Back to school, and I can't cut classes, because I'm the professor. But I know we've talked about some important things tonight, and I really hope they do you and the rest of the gnolls some good."

She nodded. "Yes. Very important."

"First, the sowing and weeding. I know this will seem

stupid to you, but humans think that because gnolls don't do any obvious damage to their territory, like plow it, or mine it, or build houses or roads or cities on it, that you're not really using the land, so it can't really be yours—and they can just come take it."

She growled ominously, and I flinched.

"Yes, I know it's stupid, but it's how most humans think. They don't understand that it's your territory—all they see is wilderness. If they see you out there pulling thornbushes, burning brush, and sowing clover and grass, they will start to view you as having some sort of claim on the land, because by altering it, you are making it yours." She looked at me dubiously. "It's not enough by itself, and many humans won't respect that claim, of course—but it will make a difference."

"We will think and talk about this," she said.

"Second, how to think 'What if...?' Do you understand what I did, talking about the zebra and the thornbush? Starting with 'I want...' or 'We want...' and asking 'How?' over and over."

She nodded. "I understand, but still very difficult. Like hunting at night in forest, not even sure for what. Hard to see, so many trees, so many shadows."

What a beautiful analogy, I thought. "You're right. You will fail almost every time. Almost always there will be no answer, or an impossible answer. But that's fine, it's just 'What if...' You can fail over and over again, and no one else has to know."

That got me a chuckle. "'Wasn't hunting, just marking territory, with bow and quiver. Also lost arrow.'"

I laughed. "Anyway, there's one big, deadly trap you can step in when playing 'What if...,' and humans step in it all the time, and you need to be extraordinarily careful not to step in it too, because it's the reason humans do a whole lot of stupid things, and this is important. You start with 'I want...,' right?"

"Yes." She nodded.

"When you want something, and you want it very, very badly—like you are so desperately hungry that you know you will die soon if you do not eat—and you ask 'How?' and there is no answer, and you ask 'How?' again and there is still no answer, or an impossible answer, it is easy to convince yourself that there really is an answer, *even if it's wrong.*"

She snorted. "Why? Say 'Giraffe kicks me, so what?' Still die when giraffe kicks."

"It's an easy trap to fall into for smaller things, though, and then the smaller things turn into bigger things very slowly, over time. 'DEATH' engraved on your sword. Praying for rain, for clear weather, for the herd to be nearby. Good luck charms, little feathers or jewelry, always with you, and since you haven't died yet, they must be working, yes?" I scowled. "Be very, very careful, because once you start convincing yourself that wanting something makes it true, *you will never stop*—and soon you'll be right there with us humans, praying instead of thinking or working, gambling because you feel lucky, paying good money to touch a 'relic' that probably got dug up from the paupers' grave, waving burning branches over the sick, and making sacrifices to Baal. So be very, very careful. Please."

Gryka laughed and laughed. "Sacrifices stupidest thing ever! *Burn meat in fire, leave hungry!*" She hooted.

"I think gnolls are more based in reality than we humans are, and I think that as predators you have to be. At least I hope so, I really do. Because once you start asking 'What if...,' you are playing inside your own head. And what's inside your own head can be strange and wonderful and even surprising, but it *isn't real,* no matter how much you wish or hope it is." I took a deep breath. "It's not real until you make it real by trying it in reality and either succeeding or failing, over and over, and not just once or twice—because that could be just luck. So please, be careful," I pleaded. "For my sake, if for no other reason, okay?"

She nodded. "Maybe better if we always play game with others. Others notice stupidity, kill it quickly."

"That helps, but others can be stupid, too. I haven't found a solution. If you do, let me know, because I can get you an associate professorship." I grinned ruefully.

Her face was as serious as I've ever seen it. "We will think and talk about this. Maybe Nako is inside his own head too much. I will ask him."

"Good. Anyway, I have to go now. The coach leaves at dawn and I still haven't packed my things." I stood up.

Gryka laughed. "Humans! Like turtles, carry whole house on back."

"I don't have fur, I need clothes. And my books and papers for work, too. You know that."

She nodded, smiling. "Yes. Still, sometimes you sound so much like gnoll, I forget. Ugly, words too big, but you understand us, mostly."

"You know that just makes me sad, Gryka." It did; my eyes were growing moist.

She rose and gave me a huge, crushing hug, which I returned as fiercely as I could. Finally we let go and stood for a time, hands on each others' shoulders.

"*Kazhda*, right?"

She nodded, eyes moist just like mine, set in that big, furry, toothy head that I had spent so many years trying to understand, and probably succeeded, and just like nearly everything else, the understanding hasn't done me a damn bit of good in the end.

"*Kazhda*."

I walked back to the inn under a bright but waning gibbous moon.

Goodbye

———

Though I usually came every summer, it had been several years since I last made the long journey to that tiny village on the northwestern frontier. The university had a reputation to uphold, I was expected to uphold mine and ours by publishing regularly, and apparently we had been succeeding because the flow of lordlings and rich bourgeois increased every year. And though I always learned so much from Gryka every time I came, I found that after the first series of visits in which we translated the Credo, I had no way to transform the rest of what I learned from her into a scholarly article that would not get me jailed or lynched. So one summer went by, and then another, and each year I intended to go back but there was always more work to be done. Finally I pushed a big pile of notes on Osengo tribal customs at my associate professors, said "Turn this into something," and began the long, bumpy, rolling sequence of carriages, riverboats, and horses that would eventually bring me back to that village, and to her.

Having finally arrived in late afternoon, I took up a spot in the village square. Some thoughtful burghers had planted a few scrawny trees, and most importantly, put up a gazebo that offered some shade against the afternoon heat. I bought a coffee and sat down to wait for news.

Nothing happened that afternoon or evening, but the next day, Nako came striding over to me, to my surprise. "Aidan O'Rourke. What do you want?" he boomed. Though still substantially taller than I am, he was smaller and more foxlike of muzzle than Gryka, and his voice carried less authority.

"Nako, I have come to see Gryka. Tell her I am here, and to come when she can."

"I will tell her, but she may not come."

I was stricken. "Why not?"

He cocked his head at me and left without replying, taking those huge strides that look so casual but cover so much ground.

That day, and the next, went by so slowly that they might have been used as torture. I swore I could hear the seconds dripping by...plink...plink...60 drips to the minute...3600 drips to the hour...I wanted to run around, scream, rip things apart, yell "GRYKA! WHERE ARE YOU?" but I knew it would do no good. So I waited.

The next morning, something happened.

I heard doors slamming, saw villagers whispering to each other and quickly shuffling home, and the few businesses that had already opened were locking their shutters and closing again. What the hell? I couldn't see a cloud in the sky, and the light breeze presaged no change in the weather.

Then I saw two gnolls enter the square and walk toward me. One was Nako again, and the other was...yes...Gryka! "GRYKA!" I yelled, jumped up, and ran to her as fast as I could, intending to knock her over with a big, fat tackle-hug, and to hell with anyone watching.

Well, I did. No one could stop me. But as I closed in, what I saw turned my joy into a strangled cry of pain and loss.

Her face and arms were covered with neat, fresh, X-shaped scars. Oh, no. No, no, no. Not only was it her *time of self-betrayal,* their number showed she was already deeply into it and very close to death. No wonder the villagers had all fled in terror. *Haouka.*

Well, if she kills me, *hazrah nachti,* I thought as I leapt, sobbing. Nako looked on with the special horror of someone who realizes that nothing he does now will be correct. And, as I expected, it was like running into a bony, furry wall...which, to my surprise, tipped over, dumping both of us in the dirt.

"You're lucky I didn't feel that or I'd bite your head off," she rumbled. I looked up through my tears at her usual lopsided grin, but even the blurriness couldn't hide the fresh, raw scars mutilating her face.

I still couldn't make any words come out. All my emotions had crashed into each other at high speed, leaving an immobile heap of wreckage. "Oh, fuck, goddamnit, Gryka."

"What? Already killed seven demon-worshippers upstream, and enough meat to feed the pack for weeks. Shitheads won't even kill me! Charge in full daylight, archers piss themselves, run like rabbits, all directions!" She laughed with a genuine pleasure that was absolutely terrifying. "Usually get one, but slowing down now. Know anything dangerous but slow?"

She grinned savagely, opening and clacking her jaws shut in the classic predator's signal of imminent aggression. There was blood on her muzzle and I smelled fresh meat. "No, I can't kill you, Aidan. You can't kill me."

Still unable to speak, I stared at her through my tears and confusion—and felt the void rise inside me once again, black, cold, infinite, and always, always hungry.

This time, though, it wasn't funny at all. *"Hazrah nachti,"* I said, with a cold vehemence that surprised even myself.

A tear rolled down her scarified cheek. She crushed me to her, and both of us sobbed like orphaned children, alone in the endless night for the first time.

Minutes or years later, the storm passed.

"It's all a big fucking lie, isn't it?" I said woodenly, staring at the ground and picking at a pebble in the dirt. "The laughter, the acceptance, that inscrutable calm, that 'We are not noble' nobility? You're just a pack of scared animals like the rest of us. The only difference is you're smart enough not to talk about it all the time—but that's not the same thing as having it beat." I picked up the pebble and flicked it at her face.

As it bounced off her big, boxy skull, I saw she was grinning—and, to my surprise, she nodded, once. "Big scared animals with big teeth and claws. Calm is easy when you're one of the scariest predators around. Try being a rabbit."

She paused. "But you're wrong. All still true. No one beats death, not even warlocks. Remember first line I wrote for you? 'We are born and we die'? I'm dying. *Hazrah nachti.* And I will die with my teeth around the biggest neck I can catch, because I will die whatever I do."

I had to agree. What else was there for a gnoll?

And what was there for me, a human? What did I intend to do before I died? Does being "human" mean anything, or does it just mean that we've lost our purpose for living and tried to substitute "bigger, better, faster, more" without knowing what we want more of—so whatever it is, it's never enough?

Gryka bounced to her feet, interrupting my reverie, and pulled me up. "Time to go."

I stared at her face, willing myself to remember every detail, but all I could see were the tears slowly making their irregular way down the tracks of her ugly, self-inflicted scars.

A thought came to me. "Can you travel three or four days south?"

"Why?"

I recalled one of the conversations I overheard during my endless trip upriver. "I've heard news that the king of Odene is raising huge work parties to build a monumentally stupid dam on the River Odene. I guess he thinks a big, stagnant lake will be more fun than the Imir Forest, and it'll also drown out the 'barbarian tribes' that their priests keep blaming for the upland drought. I don't know if there are gnolls down in the Imir, but if there are, I bet you could do some damage."

"Gnolls everywhere, even if humans don't always notice," Gryka said. Then she paused, and her grin grew wider and wider until I thought her face would split in two. "Could visit king."

Oh, shit, I thought. I was figuring she'd take out some of the trolls and ogres that were putting up the earthworks. If anyone overheard us and cared, I would be hanged, or worse, for treason.

It would *almost* be worth it. King Yerada was a pious fraud who subsidized the slave trade in order to keep his harem full of exotic catamites, publicly tortured his political enemies, and taxed outlying villages like ours into famine in order to bribe the Church into complicity.

I wondered how much of this Gryka knew—or cared about. "How the hell would you do that?"

"Assassination is only difficult if you care about living afterward." She was intently sharpening her claws against the little stone she kept on her belt.

No wiggle room on that one: I cursed inwardly. Then I shrugged: as well hanged for a sheep as for a lamb, and neither the king nor his tax collectors have many supporters out here. "Should I go with you? Do you need anything from me? Is there anything I can do to help?"

"No, stay. Faster than you, know the way. But you can help now."

I looked at her with what I later realized was a genuinely gnollish gesture of puzzlement. She fixed me with a stare so intense I could barely breathe.

"In *haouka,* our minds go fuzzy and our limbs go numb. If we wait too long, we lose all sensation and all control, and we die.

"I need pain now to bring back my mind,

and since you have given meaning to my death,

I want your marks on me when I kill the king."

Oh, no.

She handed me her belt knife. "Use toothed side. Hurts more."

As an ethnologist, I can watch any ritual, no matter how disgusting—but doing it myself is another thing entirely. "Shall I heat it and burn you? That hurts even worse." But I was really thinking that it would be easier to simply press it against her flesh than to cut into it.

"No. No time."

"Where?"

"Anywhere that hurts. Badly."

I saw her face and arms already covered with fresh scars, and wondered where I could possibly go that would hurt more but still let her travel unimpeded. Feet and legs were out, hands were out except as a last resort. Then something came to me from my misspent youth, hanging around the tattoo shop with the tough kids but not having the guts to actually get one (and glad I didn't, after seeing what some of them ended up with).

"Give me your arm, Gryka." She held it straight out. "Elbow against your body, hand up by your shoulder, don't make a fist, keep the hand loose." Fortunately gnolls are always bony, and Gryka was noticeably thinner than before.

Probably her *time of self-betrayal* left her with no appetite, I thought. And then: here I am, at one end of the village square in Northwest Bumblefuck, getting ready to deliberately saw into the flesh of my dying friend in the hopes that it would postpone her death long enough for her to assassinate the worthless King of Odene.

I held her forearm with one hand and placed the toothed side of her knife against the bony ridge of her exposed ulna, just below the wrist. The teeth were dull with use. "Ready?"

She looked at me with lust and a little fear, like a lover waiting for me to impale her on my cock.

"Do it."

I held her forearm and pulled the knife across her bone. It felt just like sawing at kindling for the fire, if I ignored the fur and the fact that I was cutting my dying friend.

She grimaced, but didn't flinch or make a noise. "Good. More."

I looked at the wound I had just opened. Thick blood was

already oozing out and matting her fur, and I could see bone in the opening. Somehow I needed to do this without weakening or destroying her arm, I thought, but the teeth were so dull that I would have to saw multiple times to damage the bone—I hoped.

I moved the knife fractionally lower, down her arm. "Ready?"

"Stop talking. Do it."

I sawed again. Still no reaction. "Again."

Down a little more, pull, nothing. "Yessssss."

Again. She growled. Her blood was flowing freely onto my off hand.

Again. She clenched her fist and barked. "One more."

A bigger one for luck. She roared like a lion, stomped her paws, and blew out a huge breath. "Now, other arm."

Just like sawing kindling. Really. Ignore my friend's blood dripping down my sweaty arms, ignore her cries of pain while she asks me to inflict more, ignore the fact that I will probably be detained and tortured if she succeeds; I had a job to do and I did it. I am proud of that.

Her other arm was worse, because each cut brought more of her back. She growled and yipped and made horrible whining wounded-animal noises, but she never flinched, ever.

Finally she pushed me away, held her hands up above her head, looked straight into the sun, shook her bloody fists at the sky, and roared loudly enough to shake dust off the neighboring merchant's roof. It was the most terrifying and beautiful image of pure defiance I have ever seen, and if the Gods were real, such a challenge ought to have brought them forth from whatever mountains, caverns, or towers they hide in while they fuck with our destiny.

That done, Gryka came to me, clawed fingers dripping blood from her wounded forearms, and hugged me like a brother—probably ruining my clothes, but I didn't care, not even a little.

"You did that well."

I wouldn't trade the memory of that single bloody hug for the riches of the Pharaohs.

She released me but still held my hands. Her eyes shone brightly with new energy, and I could see the old Gryka behind the scars, the one who wasn't dying and leaving me forever. "How long before you have to do that again?"

"Four or five days, maybe a week. Less each time."

"It'll get you to Odene, anyway. You know what I did, right?"

"Yes. Bone hurts."

"Try poking yourself with the knife point. Shin bones are good too, if you can still walk afterward."

She leaned into me and whispered in my ear: "Odene summer festival in four days, lasts four more. End is big parade, always with king and queen. Will come watch."

Still holding hands, we looked at each other, both of us grinning widely. "Help one more time, then I go. Cut yourself."

Gryka handed me the bloody knife. I was past questioning. "Where?"

"Anywhere that bleeds. Inside of arm, maybe. Get a vein, not too many."

How sensible, I thought. I held the knife in my fist like a small child holds a pencil, point protruding downward, blade flat against my palm, and made a small slash across an exposed forearm vein. Purple blood welled from the cut, mixing with her own that was already drying in the heat.

Gryka took my arm, squeezed it a few times to get the cut flowing, bent her head to it, and licked my blood away with several swipes of her huge, rough tongue. She swallowed, with obvious pleasure.

"Now you take mine." She held out a gory arm, thick blood still welling from the ragged slashes I had made. I licked her wounds, already starting to clot, and got a good mouthful of hot, warm, salty blood—and Gryka's fur. She laughed as I tried unsuccessfully to spit the fur out, gore running down my chin. "Swallow it, you."

I did. "Now what?"

"Now we know when the other dies."

"I thought that was a human kids' story."

"Human kids don't die much, and if they do, they don't tell their parents what happened."

Even dying, Gryka was full of surprises. How would she know that? How did she know about Odene's summer festival? Well, it wasn't important now. This was my last time with her, ever.

We were still holding hands. "Gryka..."

She looked at me with that puzzled look of full attention. This was the end. I wanted to get it right.

"All this pain, all this sadness, all the endless waiting and sweating here in the ass end of nowhere, even the howling void where I used to have a soul, or thought I did...

"It's been worth it, to know you. I wouldn't trade a moment of it for anything in the world. Anything."

She nodded, once, and gave me a big lopsided smile that I will remember every day until I die.

"Aidan, you are the only human that understands us, and we have work to do. You are welcome with us anytime. Nako, make this happen and tell him our plan." I had completely forgotten about Nako, who nodded in acknowledgment.

Once again she hugged me, fiercely yet briefly. "Goodbye, Aidan." It was the only time I ever heard her, or any other gnoll, use a human expression of greeting or farewell.

"Goodbye, Gryka."

Eyes clear and dry, Nako and I watched her lope southward.

"*Hazrah nachti,* eh?" Nako said.

"Shut the fuck up," I snapped. His expression was so dumbfounded that I burst into laughter. Whooping, cackling laughter. The more I laughed, the more puzzled Nako looked, and the harder I laughed. There I was, staggering through the village square, face streaked with muddy tears, clotted gore dripping from my mouth, covered in dirt and gnoll blood and human blood, howling and yipping and cackling, the gnoll beside me looking horrified, clean, and prim by comparison, and the contrast made me howl and shake and beat at the walls of the gazebo with bloody yet humorously impotent fists.

Completely out of breath, I paused for a moment, and heard (with my bones and heart, if not my ears) a distant, diminishing, yet joyfully familiar cackle, quickly traveling south.

Death

———

Gryka waited on the roof of an apartment building in Odene, four stories up, absently sawing at her shinbones with the toothed side of her belt knife, her blood dripping and congealing on the hot roof shingles.

Her arrival had caused much consternation and upheaval among the gnolls of the Imir Forest, who had not known about the dam. Since humans avoided the Imir, believing it to be the home of evil spirits as well as deadly creatures, its gnolls were not used to interacting with humans at all, much less thinking on their terms. They were primitive even for gnolls, using mostly bone knives and the occasional crude longbow made from green saplings, and they did not even have the custom of sending those in their *time of self-betrayal* to fight other packs, since they were the only pack in the Imir. *Haouka* simply went off alone to kill trolls and such until they died, and none of them had brought back the trick of extending their functional lifespan with self-mutilation.

Gryka's size and strength got her an instant measure of respect upon her arrival. When she explained her scarification to them, they fell completely silent, looking at her as though she had returned from the dead—which, to them, she had. As such, they had begun to ascribe supernatural powers to her, which she tried only halfheartedly to dispel, as she needed their help to execute her plan, and with it, the Odene king.

The part she had thought would be hardest—convincing the pack they were in danger from the dam—was easy. As one come back from the dead, Gryka was expected to know these sorts of things. The tough part was getting some idea of Odene's geography. Many Imir pack members had a habit of raiding corpses from the cemetery, inconveniently placed near the city center; but since they only went alone or in twos, and at night, no one could agree on the best or fastest route to get there, and no one had much idea where anything outside the cemetery was located.

Finally she fished out some paper, a pencil, and a gum eraser Aidan had given her, took the four or five least useless gnolls aside, and showed them a map she had previously drawn. *"This is a map. Do you know what a map is?"*

"It shows you what a place looks like when you're a bird," said a brash youngster named Natch.

"Yes. I need to draw a map of Odene. Who can help?"

From the gnolls' previous descriptions, she thought she had a fair idea of the cemetery layout: big aboveground mausoleums on the crest of the hill, rows of buried coffins and headstones below, buildings containing ashes at the bottom. Once she sketched something like that, the gnolls immediately started arguing: *"No, ash building next to stream,"* and so on. Roaring for quiet, she boomed *"Stop! Now show me where the stream ought to be."* She methodically added locations to the map, drawing and erasing, drawing and erasing, finally pulling out another sheet of paper as a fourth erasure of the Serpent Tower (everyone knew where it was, and everyone knew it was in a different place) tore through the current one.

It took an entire day for Gryka to draw something she considered usable. To test it, she had Natch narrate his route into the city from memory, and she thought she recognized the landmarks he used. Finally, as night fell, she asked *"I need two of you to sneak me into the graveyard on the last night of Summer Festival. Who will go?"*

Her guides were Natch, whose balls hadn't even dropped, and a compact young female named Thraka. Apparently sneaking to and from the graveyard was a sort of rite of passage, one that the youngsters best remembered. And Natch was clearly the sharpest arrow in the quiver...he loved making maps, and Gryka thought he could be taught to read and write.

The next three days Gryka spent resting, forcing herself to eat and drink the offerings brought to her, and meditatively cutting geometric designs into herself to stay alert. Once she awakened with both legs stuck to the ground by her own blood. She had very little time left—but it would be enough.

The long night trek into the city was remarkably uneventful. The river brought them within perhaps a half mile of the cemetery, so long as one stayed on the right tributaries (Natch had made up a little song to remember the route, which he hummed quietly to himself as they went), and the wealthy of Odene had a convenient habit of building their large private estates on the river. There were tall spiked fences to climb or jump, but those posed little trouble to a gnoll. Neither did the guard dogs of these estates, which had learned to stay near the house and away from the river lest the gnolls need a midnight snack. "What fun a pack could have here," Gryka thought, but she forced herself to concentrate. There was still much left to do.

Safely ensconced among the mausoleums, she told her escorts two things—one for each. "*Thraka, remember this well. Whether I succeed or fail tomorrow, you must go to my pack to the North. Once you arrive, tell them about your pack here in the Imir, and what has happened since I came here. I've taught you the way. Do you remember it?*"

"*Yes, I do.*"

"*Will you do it?*"

She looked scared, but met Gryka's terrible, scarred gaze without flinching. "*Yes, I will.*"

"*Good girl. Natch, you must go with Thraka. When you get to my people, tell them they must teach you to read and write, just like Nako. I've taught you the way. Do you remember?*"

For once, Natch was completely serious. "*Yes, Gryka, I remember.*"

"*Will you do it?*"

"*Yes, Gryka, I will.*"

"*Tomorrow I will die. If you hear a great commotion in the city—greater than usual—I have succeeded. If not, I have failed. Both of you must do what I told you no matter what happens. Leave me now.*"

The parade route was easy to find. The seating had been laid out the previous day, and the route started and ended at the castle, which her map miraculously showed to be approximately in the right place. Only a few fat, sleepy guards patrolled the largest of the bleachers, not really expecting to find anything but local kids necking or smearing tar on the seats, so it was no trouble for Gryka to rip away a banner and improvise a hooded cloak of sorts. It wouldn't fool anyone at less than half a block, even at night, but it would have to be enough. All she needed was a tall, convenient roof, and wasn't that what cities were for?

Apparently the parade route had been selected with at least one eye toward security, because it followed wide streets with distant buildings, all dismayingly defensible. She followed it on neighboring streets, sneaking onto the route every few blocks to look for a likely roof, with no success at all.

Finally she saw the edge of the Old City, and grinned to herself. The route took a left turn to avoid the Old City proper, but an ornate four-story hotel, complete with balconies from which minor dignitaries could watch, squatted contentedly on the inside corner, just a narrow sidewalk's width from the street.

It would be guarded, she thought, and probably swept at least once, but that was fine. If she couldn't kill and eat one fat, lazy guard, well, *hazrah nachti*. Besides, the anticipation was starting to bring back her appetite. She folded her "cloak", tucked it in her belt, and quickly shinned up an exposed drain.

The roof was tricky: strongly peaked, with gables on two sides and three dormers on the other two. In order to make the leap she planned, she would have to run lengthwise down the peak of one of them—a feat which wouldn't normally require a second thought, but in her rapidly failing state, would require some concentration.

Yet the chimney, so useless for takeoff, provided an excellent hiding place: it protruded from the side of the roof away from the street, leaving a wedge-shaped hollow between the chimney and the roof that was mostly hidden on each side by the dormers. She might not even have to eat any guards.

Gryka thought: which side to jump from? Where would the parade be slowest and closest to her? She crept over the peak and looked down at the intersection, and honestly couldn't decide...both streets were equally wide, and both the peak and the dormers gave her enough run-up to make the leap she needed. Perhaps in the daytime a strategy would suggest itself; meanwhile, it was time to rest. She unfolded the white "cloak", folded herself against the chimney, covered herself (leaving her head open to the air), and slept the light, dreamless half-sleep of one alone in hostile territory at night.

The sky lightened, gently waking her, and she licked dew off the slate roof tiles to slake her thirst. Parades weren't usually until the afternoon. It would be a long wait. That was fine.

She heard doors open and shut, followed by brisk footsteps, as the early risers began their day. As the sun rose, they were joined by the snort and clop of horses and the rumble of carriages. Finally people began to stir in the apartments under her. She heard arguments, the quiet moans of the hung-over, breakfasts being delivered and eaten.

And finally, the moment Gryka knew would come...the watch clomping up the stairs, inspecting apartments. "Palace security, milord. Are you decent?"

She could only hear two guards. That figured...there were so many buildings and roofs to check. Second floor...now the third...now the fourth, perhaps unoccupied...no, just quiet; she heard the low voice of a man talking with a guard, though she had only heard one set of footsteps. Either he hasn't moved or he walks very quietly, she thought.

"Mind if I open your dormer windows, guv'nor? Gotta check the roof."

More inaudible speech. She silently unfolded herself from the cloak and placed it gingerly under her feet, listening carefully for which window the guard would check first. Fortunately the guard's heavy boots made plenty of noise and the windows were sticky. Left dormer, she thought, I'll just hide behind the other side of the chimney.

Gryka heard the guard grunting and puffing as he hitched his torso outside so he could see out onto the roof. "Alright, then." The window closed noisily, and the guard's heavy steps trudged around to the other window. She oozed around the back of the chimney while he grunted and puffed again. "And a fine roof it is, guv. Thank you." The window slammed, the guards' heavy footsteps receded down the stairs, and she returned to her hiding place, resting and waiting, listening to the bustle of activity grow as the sun beat down, morning became afternoon, and the crowd began to gather.

Nothing more happened, but she cut and sawed at her shins and ankles a few more times to stay alert, just in case it did. She heard the parade long before she saw it.

Gryka peered over the peak of the roof, watching the King's float slowly, ponderously inch down the avenue. Easy prey, she thought, it isn't even moving at a walking pace. It's a long jump, but nothing I haven't made before. The difficult part will be landing right, so I can get up and take the killing bite before the guards realize what's happening...the float's tall, but it's still a long ways down, I can't count on killing the king by landing on him, and I'd just impale myself on that huge crown anyway, or on some of that *nerga* stuck to his throne. Now, is there any reason to wait for him to turn the corner...?

She felt the hot afternoon sun on her back, directly behind her, and thought: No, none at all. Jump from here and I'll be falling straight out of the sun. They'll be lucky if they see me at all before I land on their heads. I'll just have to resist the urge to scream as I drop.

Gryka unhooked her belt, with her loincloth and all its associated pouches, and quietly set it behind her, against the chimney. There's nothing on it I need anymore, she thought, it'll just flap around as I'm falling. I'll make this kill the clean way, with tooth and claw, and I'll die the same way I came into the world, with nothing.

The King's float inched down the block towards her. She shook out her legs in preparation, picked up her belt knife, and absently sawed at the side of her ribcage, the faint, distant sparks of pain keeping her dying, brutally scarified body awake and alert. No slipping on your own blood, she thought, as she carefully wiped her paws on the cloak and gently set the bloody knife down on it.

Thus prepared, Gryka let her focus narrow, shifting to the predator's attention, focused entirely on her prey and its immediate surroundings. The King and Queen sat on massive, jewel-encrusted thrones, swaddled in fur robes that must have weighed twenty pounds each, and occasionally lifting a limp royal wrist to wave at the obediently but limply cheering populace. A square of empty space was cleared in front of them so they could see forward, and the space beside and behind them was occupied by sweating pages, frantically fanning the King and Queen for all they were worth. They were surrounded by uniformed Royal Guards with bows and short swords, and the entire float, including the horses pulling it, was surrounded by a bristling phalanx of pikemen and mounted knights.

One choice, she thought. Land right in front and take the killing bite before those guards figure out what's happening.

The King and Queen were in line with the first dormer. Perhaps ten seconds, she thought, bouncing slightly on her legs.

The float lurched forward a few feet.

Now.

Gryka vaulted over the peaked roof and onto the peak of the center dormer on the street side. The hot slate, cooked all day by the bright Odene sun, burned the flesh of her paws, and any human without shoes would have screamed in pain and fallen—

but Gryka was long into her *time of self-betrayal,* and registered only a vague warmth as she began to run along the peak, gauging the span and fall to the King's float over three stories beneath her—

three steps, two steps, one step, SPRING out and up—

and the moment she sprang, she knew that her trajectory was correct, *nikai,* that she would land right in front of the King, and she screamed in pure predatory triumph, the full-throated battle scream of an attacking gnoll, which so few hear and live to describe—

Oops, she thought as she fell.

It turns out that human reaction time to anything completely unexpected is over half a second at the best of times. Add the stupor brought on by slowly cooking in the hot sun all day in your official dark red and black Royal Guards' uniform, with no water or piss breaks. Add the fact that the scream you are hearing is so loud, and so frankly terrifying, that you can't tell where it's coming from. Then add the fact that the screaming shape is apparently falling out of the sun and you can't see a damned thing. Finally decide you'll let an arrow fly anyway, because it's easier to explain a missed shot than why you didn't shoot—

—just about the time that the screaming shape lands behind you with a heavy WHUMP that cracks the superstructure of the whole damned float, right on top of the fucking King and Queen, the queen's throne is knocked sideways but she looks alright, oh Christ what is that huge hellbeast in front of the King, it's trying to kiss him or something—

Gryka landed tall on her legs, absorbed the impact with a perfect shoulder roll, and sprang to her feet grinning, right in front of the begowned, bejeweled, becrowned, fat, sweaty, and utterly dumbfounded king. One wickedly clawed hand knocked the tall, heavy crown off his balding head, and as she bent to him, she noticed its pleasingly small size. Another change in plans, she thought, opened her jaws around the king's entire skull, and bit down hard, crushing it like a tomato just as the first short sword sliced into her body.

The guards hacked at her again and again, swords biting deeply, but the pain of half-severed limbs was bee stings and paper cuts to her dying, spent body as she chewed the king's delicious brain. Finally she swallowed a bite and managed one last convulsive, coughing laugh, spraying the vomiting guards with bone chips, gray matter, and hamburger as she died.

Gryka's last thought: *Nikai.* Thanks, Aidan. Now I can rest.

And no matter how hard the guards hacked at her lifeless, bleeding, brutally scarified body, they couldn't cut the bloody, misshapen grin off Gryka's face, or out of their own minds.

———

I was on a boat drifting lazily downriver, stripping maple seeds that had fallen on deck and sticking them on the railing every few inches, making it look like the entire aft deck had grown wings or been invaded by locusts. It was the final day of Odene's summer festival, and though I was sure the whole "blood brothers" ritual was a shuck, I couldn't stop thinking about Gryka and what she might be doing—or might be done to her—right now.

Suddenly my gut tied itself in knots, my bones went cold, and I knew, absolutely knew, that Gryka was dying right now, just as surely as if she were dying in front of me. Tell me, I implored. Did you make it? Did you do it? Tell me if you can, Gryka. Please.

The coldness passed, and was replaced by a terrible serenity. Yes, death is serene, I know that. Especially for you, who denied it for so long and with so much pain. I'm happy for you, Gryka. But did you kill the king?

Though I hadn't eaten for hours, I noticed a distinct taste in my mouth. Blood. Had I bit my lip? No, there was more to it than that. A bit sweet, a bit gelatinous, very rich and fatty, delicious. And the crunchy, chalky tang of...calcium?

Realization dawned. I grinned.

Then I laughed.

Then I danced a little reel, right there on the aft deck.

Then I yelled for the captain. "Change in plans, Sammy. I'm going to Odene."

"Sure you want to get off near Odene? Summer Festival ends today, and for a week no one does anything but nurse hangovers and clean up trash."

"Yes, I'm sure. I heard there's something special happening this year."

"Suit y'self."

———

Later that night, I poured out a fifth of very expensive whiskey on the river, and spoke aloud. "I never promised you this while you were alive, Gryka, but I promise it now. Fuck *hazrah nachti*, your story is worth telling, and I'll tell what I know of it."

So I did.

Epilogue

Bicycle

——

Gryka can run much faster than I can, because digitigrade legs are so much more efficient than ours. A full-speed sprint for me is a casual jog for her, and I have to jog just to keep up with her walk. It's hard for us to travel together. Parents with small children know what this is like. So I decided to take Gryka on a mountain bike ride with me, because maybe on the downhills I can outpace her.

She eyed my bicycle skeptically as I rolled up. "Complicated. Looks *nerga*."

"Actually, it's very simple, compared to most human stuff. No decoration, everything has a function. Turn pedals, pulls chain, turns rear wheel, bike goes forward, right?" I lifted the rear wheel and turned the cranks by hand. The rear wheel spun up, and the hub buzzed as I let go.

She nodded. "Yes."

"Butt on seat, feet on pedals, hands on grips, yes? Now watch." I had spent so much time with her that I was starting to talk like her. "See this lever? Squeeze it."

She reached forward with one big, blocky hand and tried to grab the lever itself. "No, hold the grip and the lever, squeeze them together."

The bike jumped as the rear wheel stopped instantly. Gryka's eyes narrowed. "Wheel stops. How?"

I put the rear wheel down. "See cable, coming from lever? Squeeze lever, pulls cable. Cable goes to rear brake, so." I traced its path down the frame tubes to the rear disc, and squeezed it so she could see the rear brake arm move.

Her face lit up. "Like tendon! Move muscle, pulls tendon, attached to bone, moves arm, leg!"

"Right. Now look inside the brake, hard to see, but watch. Pads pinch together when I pull, grab this disc, stop the wheel." I pantomimed this, using the thumb and fingers of one hand to grab the disc. Then I squeezed the lever again.

She nodded. "Clever! But you and bike are heavy, move fast. Squeeze lever, one finger, easy. How does bike stop?"

Great. Now I have to explain leverage to a gnoll. "You understand leverage, Gryka?"

"Don't know word. Explain."

"The brake lever moves this much, right?" I held my thumb and finger an inch apart. "How far does the brake pad move?"

She peered intently at the mechanism. "Maybe a few hairs."

"Yes, it hardly moves at all. But there is the same power in both motions."

Her face showed such an effort of concentration that I laughed. "Okay, I need to think of another example. Aha!" I grinned hugely: I was learning to think like she did. "Gryka, when you need to crunch a really big bone, like a thighbone, what do you do?"

"Bite it. Goes in mouth." She gave me a sour look.

"Right, of course, but where in your mouth?"

"In back. Easier that way."

"But why?" I pounced. "Same muscles, front teeth are even sharper. Why is it easier in back?"

I gave her a little while, but she still looked puzzled.

"Open your mouth. How far do your front teeth move, and how far do your back teeth move?"

She yawned, her long muzzle exposing a truly imposing set of teeth; incisors, fangs, premolars, carnassials, all shaped to slice and tear and crush every part of my body into small, easily-digestible chunks. "Front teeth move more. Lots more." Wide enough to fit my head in there, probably.

"But same muscles, right? No more power. Just less movement. You see?"

"I know, but I don't see. Fast prey."

So close, yet so far. "The hell with it. Let's go. Follow me."

Grinding uphill, endless uphill. She would disappear some distance up the trail, then wait for me and laugh. "Slow! You run faster! Why bring machine?"

"Just you wait," I puffed, breathing hard. "We're almost to the top." She ran ahead again.

We looked out over the valley and the lake. It was beautiful, and pleasantly cool at altitude. "You have good endurance," Gryka complimented me. "Too slow, though."

"Humans hunted like you do, usually. Ran prey to exhaustion. Needed better trackers, though; we were too slow to keep prey in sight."

She nodded. "More difficult. Maybe why you got smarter, faster, than gnolls did."

I thought about this as I fastened my helmet. "I think you're right. We needed the brains to make up for being slower and weaker. Our scientists think they went together. Ever notice how humans look a lot like baby chimpanzees?"

Gryka hooted with laughter. "Baby chimps! Yes!"

"But not adult chimps, right?"

She was still chuckling, but managed a reply. "Less. Still ape, though."

"Right. Baby chimps. Big head, but small and weak, right? We think we got the brains from simply not growing up all the way, and the brains we got from the big head were more important than getting slower and weaker. If you're smart enough to make a knife or spear, that's much more important than being a little bit faster or stronger. Nice to take one or the other, but no choice, right?"

Gryka nodded. "Like choosing mate. Male fast, strong, a little dumb. Can't say 'Give me fast, strong cub like you, but keep my brains.'"

"Right. Anyway, the two went together, and we had to take both. Apes aren't very good hunters, so it probably didn't matter so much to us. Making tools was much more important."

I never saw Gryka "lost in thought" like a human—her attention never turned completely inward—but she was thinking hard about this. "I see now. Cruel choice. Remember easy life in trees, but can't go back."

I nodded, sadly. "We have stories about that. Stories so old that most people have forgotten that's what they really mean." We can't go back to the Garden of Eden, and it wasn't the fruit of knowledge at all...I laughed. Oh, this is beautiful, I thought.

"Meat, Gryka! It wasn't fruit in the Garden of Eden, it was *meat!* It's nice, sitting in trees all day, eating fruit and nuts and bugs in the shade, but there's no *meat!* Every so often our distant ancestors got lucky, caught a little monkey or a baby pig or something else small, and their meat is delicious and fills you up like nothing else—but they're hard to catch, and they're tiny. And you're looking out from the edge of the forest, over the grasslands, and what do you see but huge, thundering, earth-shaking herds of MEAT! Striped meat, spotted meat, black meat, yellow meat, meat with fur and hide and hooves and horns and tails and manes and you can *smell* it from the edge of the forest, walking, running, drinking, eating, having babies, every possible size, shape, color, texture, and configuration of DELICIOUS MEAT! *AND YOU CAN'T HAVE ANY!*"

I was shouting at her at the top of my voice, and she was howling and shaking with laughter, and that was good and that was right because I was speaking Truth and if I've learned anything at all in my time with Gryka, it's that it is not just possible for Truth to be funny and serious at the same time, it is *absolutely mandatory.*

"And you drool to yourself a little bit and you think, 'Well, it sure is nice and comfortable up here in this tree, and I sure do like nuts and mangoes,' but that smell has worked its way into your brain, and you know, you absolutely *know,* that those tiny little monkeys, as tasty as they are, are nothing, *nothing* compared to the taste of the endless delicious banquet laid out before you on the grasslands, you can see it and smell it, table after table after table, and the other apes are all a-flutter, 'No, it's dangerous, don't go down there, you'll be killed!' and you roar back 'No! NO! I am fucking *hungry,* and that is some *delicious fucking food* right down there, and you know it and I know it, and I am going to march down there, into the mud and the shit and the fear and the blood and the dying, and I am going to *GET. ME. SOME. FUCKING. MEAT!*"

Gryka was laughing so hard she was crying. "Yes! Yes! You understand!"

"And that, Gryka, is why humans are so screwed up. We want meat, but we want to go back to the trees, too, so we go back and forth and back and forth, never content, never stopping. Writing beautiful symphonies, torturing heretics, building schools and universities, building atomic bombs, saving children, raping children, save the planet, kick the dog. And understanding a problem is *not* the same thing as solving it, but it's the first step, and I have taken it. And I am going to take the next step, which is to say this: Go back to the trees if you want, go back to the Garden of Eden and lie there and eat your fucking mangoes, but we all know what is going to happen there, which is this: someday the trees will burn or fall or be cut down by those who left the Garden before you, and you will be thrust down here into the mud and the shit and the blood and the dying, and *you will know fear*—but only for about five minutes, because the teeth and the claws will surround you and boy, do all those mangoes make your blood taste sweet and you will all die very, very quickly, but not quickly enough, because being ripped apart by those teeth and those claws will seem like forever. *The End.*"

I paused and took a deep breath. "And I will continue: Fellow humans, this leaves us with one choice, so we must make it, and we must make it now. And that is to accept that we are now down here with the predators, and we are now predators ourselves, and we cannot go back to the Garden. And we must also accept the fact, the silly, tragic accident, that we are *bad predators*. Terrible. The worst. We need knives, guns, trucks, and highways to do what a scruffy little coyote can do with its own teeth and claws—and now that we've made enough technology to kill things by remote control, the joy of the hunt is gone." I growled. "We can hunt everything to extinction and still not feel it. Shark's fin soup, leopard-skin coats, bear-skin rugs, rhino horns, tiger bones! *Timed game feeders!*"

"Sit on ass, hope prey *walks by*. Crook finger, prey dies. Keep head and horns, leave meat to rot." Gryka snorted. "Not hunting."

I nodded. "Even worse, pay others to hunt for you. Buy it in a market, or order it in a restaurant. But it's the only choice we had," I explained. "Big tool-making brains were just barely more of a survival advantage than everything else we lost. *Hazrah nachti.* But we must accept that, and embrace it, and most important of all, *we must work to improve it.*"

"Yes!" Gryka laughed. "Time to stop complaining, start hunting."

"Complaining's easier." I shrugged, grinning ruefully. "Seriously. 'Plan before hunting,' right?"

She nodded. "All so obvious to gnolls, though."

I cuffed her. "No fair. Gnolls have always been hunters. Your bad ideas starve in about two weeks. Once humans started farming, we had an entire growing season to dream up *nerga*, convince ourselves it makes the rains come."

"*Hazrah nachti.* What now?"

"Well, first we have to stop denying the obvious. We must stop believing that we can all go back to the trees and be peaceful, placid vegetarians, and that it's *our fault* when we can't. Our ancestors came down and became hunters a long, long time ago, that choice is what made us into humans in the first place, and the ones that stayed are still up there with the other gorillas and bonobos and chimps, getting shot for bushmeat." I scowled. "We can't go back, Gryka. It only takes one predator to destroy utopia."

Gryka grinned, drooling. "Utopias are delicious! *Taste like chicken.*"

And at that, I whooped with laughter, losing it so completely that I staggered into her before catching my breath.

"You're right, they do. Renounce violence, beat your swords into plowshares, turn in your guns, and either the predators eat you, or the shepherds shear you and then eat you—while telling you that it's good and natural and patriotic to be shorn and eaten, and you are a *bad person* if you object." I snorted. "If we want freedom, the only way is to be smart enough, strong enough, and fierce enough to take it and keep it."

"Only way to have anything, ever," she said, nodding. "Hyenas carrying signs, chanting! 'Lions! Stop taking our kills!' 'Hyena rights!'" She snorted. "Call packmates, bite lions back."

"That's dangerous, though, Gryka. So many humans are scared, want shepherds to protect them." I shrugged. "The shepherds say 'Sure, we'll defend you from all those nasty predators. No more monsters coming to eat you in the night, you're safe with us. In fact,' they say, grinning big, suspiciously toothy grins, 'you have no choice, because we're taking your guns and knives and chemistry sets away, *for your safety,* and we're censoring your news and books and Internet, *for your safety,* and we're tracking your cell phones and reading your texts and emails, *for your safety,* and forcing you to earn and use money that we print for ourselves whenever we need more.'" I snorted. "'But your life is much better here, inside our fence where we milk you dry every day, and we *promise* that we're not eating you as often as those scary predators,' they say, giggling, 'because we're *good shepherds.* And please don't suggest otherwise, because that makes you a *bad person,* and never, never fight back, because that makes you a *terrorist,* and bad people and terrorists *get eaten,*' and they laugh and laugh and we can see the bloody flesh stuck between their *sharp carnassial teeth."* I sighed. "And that's the second thing. There's no short cut, no easy way. No one can give us freedom or happiness—because *anyone with the power to protect us has the power to kill or enslave us,* too."

Gryka nodded. "Why gnolls have no guards, no army, no police. All armed, all train, all fight. Humans used to, but you're forgetting how."

"It's because the shepherds, the exploiters, the humans in robes and suits and uniforms who already understand all this —they teach us from birth to act like cattle *so they can keep eating us!* We learn, live, and work in tiny little pens, like cattle in a feedlot, and eat cattle food, like corn and soybeans, and travel in huge traffic-jam subway-car herds nose to tail like cattle, and we're clean and fat and comfortable and totally, desperately unhappy, because that's not freedom and *we know it."*

I scowled. "Humans are hunters, humans are predators, and if we want freedom and happiness, we must be smart enough and strong enough and fierce enough to take them and keep them. We must become *better predators* in every way—mentally, culturally, and even physically, because our physical evolution has left us in a strange transitional state with our minds so far ahead of our bodies. And this means we have a truly monstrous, unimaginably vast amount of work to do, and it will take us generations, and I barely even know where to start. We will try many, many things, some will survive and most will die, *hazrah nachti.* But even if the full effort of my entire life does not measurably diminish the work to be done, I must do it anyway. Humans must do it anyway—because we have *no choice at all*."

Gryka grinned. "Why so angry? Easy choice! Being predator is great! You hunt, and at end of hunt, you eat meat! Two best things ever!"

"Easy for you to say, Gryka. You were never in the Garden of Eden. It's nice there." I sighed. "But we can't go back."

"Then come with us!" She bounced on her paws. "Easier in pack, yes? Remind you when you forget. Run now, cold up here. Go!"

And with that, she bounded away, down the trail. I jumped on my bike, spun the cranks, and took off after her.

She was fast, scary fast, and I didn't even see her for a minute or two. But gravity is much kinder to wheels than to feet or paws, and I slowly began to reel her in. She was so graceful to watch—jumping from rock to rock, pushing off trees in corners, flowing like water—but I had my own traction to worry about. Finally I caught up to her in a section of sharp babyheads—tough as her paws were, she still had to be slow and careful on the strangely angled rocks—and yelled "Ha! Gotcha! Let me pass, now you chase!"

She laughed and dropped off the side of the trail. I upshifted two gears, stood up, and jammed it down the rest of the sharp rocks, knowing this was my chance to open up a lead. Elbows up, arms loose, look through the turn, flow like water over the rocks and roots, sweep left, up the quick little rocky chute, bump bump bump down the ragged stone steps on the backside, hard right, log drop to a long sidehill, jump the water diversions, open it up through the long sweepers around the meadow, back into the trees...I am fast, I am flowing, I am invincible! Finally the slope lets up and the trail gets wide and sandy and I start bogging down a little bit and WHAM! I go over in a flailing, churning pile of fur, claws, elbows, tires, and flying sand, which seems to take an inordinately long time to stop. And it's laughing.

Ouch.

I'm lying on my side, mostly, in the sand, and Gryka has me trapped in a bear hug. I can feel her hot breath on the back of my neck, and feel her body shaking as she laughs and laughs and I am nearly deafened as she lets out a huge, primal roar right next to my ear, and I realize I'm laughing too as I spit sand out of my mouth and try to turn around, but suddenly she has clamped down with her arms and I feel her teeth around my neck, fangs digging in and I go stiff with sudden, stark terror because I have triggered her hunting instinct and she is going to bite my head off and eat me right here in the sand and just as I start to scream, she rolls me on top of her and pushes me, hard, and I am suddenly on my feet and I turn around and scream "WHAT THE FUCK?" as I overbalance and fall back on my ass facing her and she is pointing at me and howling with helpless laughter and pounding the ground with her other big, blocky fist, and she's completely gray with dust and I've just gone from triumph to pain to laughter to terror in the space of about six seconds and everything is so completely out of control that I start laughing again, too.

We giggled for a while, like dieseling cars, and finally staggered to our feet, slapping dust and sand off of ourselves in huge, choking clouds. "Gryka, I really thought you were going to kill me for a moment, there."

She grinned a huge, lopsided grin. "Great joke! The best."

"If 'best' means 'most likely to make me die of a heart attack,' then yes." I grinned to let her know she was right, really. "Just promise not to do that when we ride again, OK? I'll get tense and ride like crap if I'm worried about you tackling me around every corner."

She nodded. "Also, not funny if you expect it. Joke is surprise. Biggest surprise, best joke."

Something big hit me, then. "Gryka, I understand something else now. For gnolls, death is funny. Something to be avoided, yes, but it's the punchline to life."

That got me one of her rare, inscrutable, sphinx-like looks: I went on. "*Haouka,* right? You know when you're getting old and dying, so you seek it out on your own, pushing harder and harder, doing bigger and better and crazier deeds until you take on something too big and it kills you. It's like you see Death coming for you, so you walk right up to him and say 'Hey, instead of playing that stupid game where I pretend I'm not dying and you won't ever catch me, how about we both go out tonight and *fuck shit up!*' And Death pulls a little flask out of his robe, uncaps it, takes a snort, and he hands it to you and you take a snort and it's hot and pungent and delicious, like fine whiskey mixed with fresh blood, and he nods, once —and then he slowly breaks into a big shit-eating grin, throws his bony arm around your shoulders and says 'Now let's go get some things *done!*'"

She was still giving me that inscrutable look.

"Anyway. We're taught that death is always horrible, never funny, can never be funny, is to be avoided at all costs—and it always finds us anyway, cowering under the bed or in the closet." I sighed. "Humans don't live any longer than gnolls do, really...it's just that *haouka* lasts thirty or forty years for us, instead of perhaps one or two for you, and by the time we're forced to admit that we're not going to live forever and we're never going to be young again, we're too old and weak and stupid to do anything about it! We act like the entire point of life is to live long enough that your kids have to feed you and cart you around like a baby, which they probably won't so you're left to die alone and confused with strangers, and that is *not funny at all*. We can't laugh at life, because we've devoted all of our energy to making sure our lives are terrible jokes with too long of a setup and no punchline."

"Never understood that," Gryka said, obviously puzzled. "So much fun to be *haouka*. Take big risks, make big kills, best thing ever!"

"Like kings." I nodded, grinning.

"Ate his brain!" She roared with laughter. "Humans! Rather lie in bed losing hair, teeth, mind. Why?"

"I don't know. Maybe farming for a few thousand years made us stupid. We know it shrunk our brains."

"Watching ox's ass all day." She snorted. "Probably better to be stupid."

I nodded. "Also, grains aren't as nutritious as meat, and we need animal fat to make our brains out of. But even farmers hunt for fun, or do things that are really just hunting, like sports."

Gryka laughed. "Why not just drop plow, go hunt again?"

"Our babies are too weak and helpless. You can leave your cubs in tunnels for days at a time while you hunt, maybe leave a couple packmates to guard them. A human mother has to carry her baby around all the time."

She thought about this for a moment. "Slows pack down. Also, mothers can't hunt."

I nodded. "That's probably why humans can still eat plants. Even a woman carrying her baby can still find fruit, dig tubers while men hunt. More importantly, though, hunter mothers can't have another child until the first is big enough to keep up, and that takes years for us. But a farmer's wife can have children one after the other because she doesn't have to go anywhere. Human hunters might be smarter, but the farmers outnumber us and breed too quickly."

She chuckled. "Poor humans. Your blood fights itself. Hunters who still want to be tree-dwellers who are best at farming, but hate it."

And there it was: the human dilemma. Once again, Gryka expressed in a few short sentences what had taken me years to puzzle out.

I laughed and shook my head. "You're right. Humans must choose one of those things, or we will be forever unhappy, tearing ourselves apart until we do. We already know we can't go back to the trees, so it's hunting or farming."

Gryka snorted. "Easy choice! Farming is stupid."

"But it works so well for us! Farmers can breed so much faster, and we're helpless without our tools anyway. Remember, we traded away everything else for our big tool-using brains. You've still got your teeth and claws."

"You already decided, Aidan. Make humans better predators."

"Well, of course." I grinned. "Humans have hunted for millions of years. It's in our blood, which is to say that we have evolved, been selected for our hunting skills, shaped to be better hunters, for millions of years. *Hunting is the song of our blood.*"

Gryka nodded fiercely.

"And that is not a poetic metaphor, that is *hard reality,* because we can read the words of that song in the form of a double helix that twists through every cell in our bodies. A few thousand years of farming isn't enough to change that."

I sighed. "Our blood calls to us, Gryka. Everything human males do for fun is hunting or war or finding mates. Racing? Chasing prey. Team sports? Chasing prey and war at the same time. Climbing mountains, running rivers, getting from here to there in the hardest, most pointless way possible, and when we're done we all go eat a big pizza like we just killed it."

Gryka howled with laughter. "So true!"

"And if we can't do it ourselves, we watch others do it, or play video games about it." I chuckled ruefully. "Even knowledge. Learning and solving problems is just hunting with your mind, hunting for knowledge. You taught me that." She nodded. "But farming isn't about inventing or making discoveries; farming is about never having to discover anything, ever. Just back and forth over the same field, pushing the same paper across your cubicle, working the same assembly line, day after day, year after year." I scowled. "We hate endless repetitive tasks, call them 'mind-numbing'—because that's not what our minds are *for!*" And I jabbed a finger at my delicate, oversized human skull. "Humans don't need these huge damned brains to *dig potatoes!* We need them to make tools and work together, so we can find, outwit, and kill animals that are much bigger, faster, and stronger than us. We need brains to *hunt.*"

"Hunters have to be smart. Every hunt is different," said Gryka. "Never know exactly where prey is, what it will do when we chase."

"Exactly! Plants don't run away, run in herds, protect their young, fight back with horns and hooves. What makes a good farmer? *Persistence and stupidity.* Put your hands to the plow and never look back. Never wonder what it would be like to stand on top of the mountain you can see from your little hut, never let yourself notice the birds calling or the antelope mating or the sun setting through clouds or the smell of a thunderstorm, because you'll plow a crooked furrow—and never, ever go swimming or prank your packmate or write a poem or practice your archery or take a nap on a rock in the sun, because there's *no time!* There's work to do, cows to milk, fences to mend, that field won't weed itself, boy, *get back to work,*" I growled. "And if you wake up early enough and work hard enough and nothing breaks or gets sick that day, maybe you can take the dogs and the shotgun and spend a few minutes around sunset doing what your blood calls you to do."

Gryka laughed. "Humans! Why work so hard, growing plants, protecting stupid cattle with fences? Prey eats plants for us, has babies for us, babies grow up, get big and fat and delicious, all for us!" She grinned, drooling.

I had never thought of it like that. Why, indeed? We domesticate animals so they're slow and stupid, easy for us to keep and kill—and then we have to spend all our time and energy defending them from other predators, feeding them, breeding them, shoveling their shit, keeping them alive because they're too weak and stupid to live without our help. Why not become hunters again, and let the entire world be our all-meat buffet?

"Plenty of time to nap, swim, practice archery, even learn reading and writing, human *nerga*. Then we get hungry again, hunt, eat meat!" She smiled. "Good life, Aidan. Why we're so fierce, protecting it."

I sighed. "You're right, Gryka, and that's the best reason of all: gnolls do have a good life. How many humans can say that, really? Life is miserable for most of us, and the lucky few who have electricity and antibiotics and indoor plumbing and enough to eat are always wanting what we don't have, no matter how much we do have, and you said why so much better than I did: *our blood fights itself.* So we're told that we're all supposed to be farmers now, that the song of our blood is just some old, embarrassing *nerga* we can give away now that we're grown up, like a child's tricycle, and we're done evolving and humans are perfect and we'll never need to change or learn anything new ever again."

I scowled. "But even if we can somehow silence the song of our blood—which we can't, all we can do is drown it out with *nerga*—that silence will be *the death of the human race*, because the world is always changing and we won't know what to do about it. We'll just keep shuffling paper back and forth, following the ox, head down, hands to the plow, as the world burns and withers around us and we die."

"Also, farmers always slaves," Gryka said.

"What?" I never got used to Gryka's abrupt topic shifts. "Slaves to ox, maybe."

She got very serious. "No. Farmers are slaves to other humans. Always."

"I don't understand."

"Farmer has house, land, crops, yes? Maybe a few pigs, sheep, cows?"

"Sure."

"King's army comes, says 'Give us half your crops and animals or we kill you. Fight or run away, we take everything. Burn house, kill anyone left behind, maybe rape instead, take as slaves.' Death or slavery for farmers, always." She snorted.

Sounds like most of human history, I thought to myself. Even today, our government sends us to prison to get raped, and we laugh about it. "I think I see, Gryka. Once you settle down, tie your survival to one small place that you have to spend lots of time making right for you, anyone else can come and threaten to destroy it. Then you're doomed, because it's so much easier to destroy things than to build them."

"Not just crops, Aidan, anything! You need *nerga* to live? 'Do what I say or I burn your *nerga*.' Or take for myself,

whatever. Humans need *nerga* to live, humans always slaves."
She snorted again.

"But how do we defend ourselves? We can't just go back to
smoke signals and stone-tipped spears," I protested. "Armies
with guns and tanks and radios will slaughter us like cattle, even
if they can't enslave us. But we can't make firearms out of bone
and sinew, either, and we can't keep hunting for knowledge
without a way to talk to each other over distances, share what
we've learned, and remember more than fits in our heads."

"Don't need to farm to make weapons." She shrugged.
"Also, hunters don't need so much *nerga*."

Apparently my puzzled look was obvious: she reached out
and tapped my smartphone with a very sharp claw. "Fits on
belt, yes? Soon, in head. Weapon, fits on back." She laughed.
"Everything else, just shiny *nerga* for houses, toys for playing
at hunting or battle, tools for making more *nerga*."

"Or cars and trucks to carry it all around," I added, slowly
beginning to understand. "You were right, before, when you
said humans are turtles. We go everywhere in our shells, can't
live outside them. Houses, cars, offices. Closets full of shoes and
clothing, *just to go outside*. Working all our lives to buy bigger,
flashier, more expensive shells, or decorate the ones we have."

And then I realized: "Gryka, we're destroying everything
we love about the Earth, our home, in order to build our
protective shells. We're remaking the world into someplace
safe and comfortable for humans...*and we don't even like the
world we're making!* We want to live in natural beauty, but we
can't survive there unaided—so we build roads to get to it,
and houses to live in it. Then, since we've forgotten how to
hunt, we cut the trees for farmland, kill the other predators to
keep our cows and pigs and chickens safe, build factories to
make clothes and cars and toys, build strip malls to sell them
to each other, foul the air and water with smog and trash and

sewage and poison—and then it's not beautiful anymore, so we go find another beautiful place and start destroying *that*."

"So much work! Makes head hurt, just to watch." Gryka chuckled. "Much easier, more fun to be gnolls. We use tools, but we don't need them to live."

I nodded. "That's the problem, right there. Humans first made tools to help us hunt, millions of years ago—but now our tools own *us,* because we can't survive without them anymore. We're not just slaves to other humans; we're slaves to our own technology. If even a small part of human infrastructure breaks, everything stops working, and if it stays broken, we start dying."

And finally I really, truly understood what has to be done. We've been struggling with the problem for hundreds of years without getting any closer to a solution, and it's because we still assume humans are perfect, finished. "Gryka, instead of working so hard to remake the world, and hating what we've made when we succeed, *why not remake humans instead?* Why not become something that can live a full, free, joyous life in the world *as it is,* as we know we want it to be?"

"More like gnolls, yes?" Gryka grinned.

"Except for the genitals, maybe," I said skeptically.

She cuffed me, hard, laughing. "Jealous male!"

I shrugged, grinning. "Probably. But you're right: we have to make ourselves into something more like you, something that can live, hunt, and be happy without our tools, without technology. Then we can be its masters, not its slaves, and it'll be something we invent and use for the joy of play and discovery—not a lifeboat that drowns us when it sinks. Sure, we'll still need to defend ourselves and hunt for knowledge, but like you said, those tools fit on a belt and on our back."

Gryka nodded. "Also, humans can cheat, change themselves. Gnolls have to breed, tiny changes take generations."

"Not quite...we don't understand enough about genetics and developmental biology. We're working on it, but it's a hard problem. Maybe the hardest." I sighed. "It's so frustrating, Gryka. We can hear the song of our blood, but we can't heed it—yet. We're caught halfway, still trying to fight our way out of slavery."

And I thought about hiking through what's left of wilderness with my friends, forty pounds of tents and stoves and food and clothes and sleeping bags lashed to our backs like turtle shells...how it's still so much better than sitting in our cubicles all day, hands to the plow, following the ox, so we can earn the money to buy all that gear on our backs...and how it would be to live and learn and teach and hunt and love and simply *wake up* in that absolute, jaw-dropping beauty, every day, without carrying that weight—

—and without even wanting what it contains.

"Most important thing ever, for humans," she said, very seriously. "Slaves to *nerga*, slaves to each other. No good."

"I think that's why I envy the gnolls so much, Gryka. Sure, your life is short, dangerous, and bloody—but you're as free as anyone can ever be."

She shrugged. "Freedom is dangerous. You want safety? Sure, I'll keep you safe," she said as she brought herself up to her full height, fur bristling, towering over me. "One thing first, though." And she slowly grinned a huge, symmetrical, predatory grin.

I think I knew what was coming, but she roared it so fiercely that I cringed anyway.

"LICK MY BALLS!"

Both of us exploded into howling laughter, staggering like drunks, leaning against each other for support as we gasped like fish.

Somehow, Gryka caught enough breath to fix me with another big predatory grin. "Didn't lick right! KILLING YOU ANYWAY!"

And with that, I lost it completely, collapsing helplessly onto the sand, dragging her down with me as the storm bore us away, finally washing us ashore, still shaking with giggles.

Gryka's right, I thought. That's our life as modern humans, right there—and unless we can become self-sufficient hunters, become the true predators our blood tells us we are, licking the balls of authority is the best we can hope for, and we're doomed to the Orwellian future of a boot stomping on our face, forever.

Something else hit me then, as we lay in the sand, still chuckling. "I bet that's where religion came from, the whole idea of heaven and hell, eternal reward, eternal punishment. Even farmers know that life is supposed to be more than than humiliation, slavery, and death, but they don't know what to do about it—so they make up stories about life after death, in paradise."

Gryka shrugged as we disentangled ourselves and stood up. "Maybe."

"But then the sharp-toothed shepherds said 'Aha! We can use those stories. We'll tell our subjects 'Sure, you go to Paradise after you die.' Cheaper than feeding them, words are free." Gryka laughed. "'But,' say the kings, the priests, the politicians, 'you only go to Paradise if you're a *good, obedient sheep*. Ask too many questions, fight back, you are a *bad person* and you go to HELL! Eternal punishment!' they howl."

I scowled. "'The Lord is my Shepherd, I shall not want.' 'Muslim' means 'One who submits.' You are helpless, you are prey, you are MEAT! Could it be *any more obvious?*"

"Why ask me?" Gryka said, laughing.

"I know, rhetorical question. *But we believe it anyway!* We live our entire sad little lives afraid, terrified! to eat the wrong food, or do the wrong thing on the wrong day, or see someone's tits or dick or even think about it too much, or dance, or sing, or forget to turn towards God's ass and kiss it five times a day, or put the wrong flowers on the wrong statue, or tell our worthless husband or useless wife to fuck off and get out, and especially, especially never to think that it might all be a giant multi-century con job by the shepherds, the exploiters and enslavers, whose real purpose is to keep us from taking our life and our freedom back from them, today, right now.

"So now you are dying, having shouted down the song of your blood with a lifetime of constant pain and suffering and self-denial, and you're finally expecting that big proud A+, gold star, go to the head of the class, up through the pearly gates, 72 virgins waiting for you, and the blackness is descending and the lights are going out and you are still waiting, and it's getting darker and darker and the doubt is gnawing and gnawing and finally you know, absolutely *know,* that this is it. You only get one life, and you were tricked into *giving it away,*" I growled, "and you get one terrible instant of pure, total, complete rage and pain and loss and failure and regret just before the lights go out. Curtain."

I was fuming, and Gryka was...crying? Big, fast tears. She threw her head back and howled, a horrible, sad, lonely keening, not like a wolf at all, no, like dying alone and in pain. I stepped forward and hugged her as hard as I could, and she threw her arms around me like she was drowning and she keened and howled and it was such a desolate, painful sound that I started to cry a little too.

The worst of the storm passed, and she pulled her head back to look at me. "So sad. Didn't know. Always thought you were just defective human. Thought humans liked working and suffering and dying for big men in funny hats and clothes. Like ants or bees, work for queen."

"No, we hate it, Gryka. We hate it worse than anything. But we do it because we think that's what humans are for and we'll be punished forever if we don't. We even feel bad because we don't like it and we think we're supposed to."

With that, her eyes got narrow and hard. "Then you have task. Big task."

"I have a lot of tasks, remember? Put it on my list, I'll get back to you." She cuffed me, laughing. "No, you're right, it's important, but it's just the first step of a very long journey towards becoming *better predators,* and that journey never ends. And that's part of everything you've taught me and everything I've learned by talking with you and laughing and crying and getting tackled and slashed and every other strange and terrible and beautiful thing that we've done together. And I'm going to tell everyone *every single thing.*"

She gave me a skeptical look. "Even boring parts?"

I laughed. "No, I'll skip those. But I can't skip anything else. It means too much to me. You mean too much to me." She cuffed me again, then hugged me.

I heard clanking noises in the distance. "Hey, let me move my bike. Riders coming." We let each other go, and I pulled my bike off the trail. The front wheel was turned around and I lost a bar end cap, but aside from the dust, everything seemed to be fine.

"You okay?" the lead rider asked as he coasted past in a cloud of dust, hubs buzzing.

"Never better," I yelled back.

"Race you to the car," I said, but Gryka was gone.

———

I still remember what she said at the top of the mountain. "Then come with us! Easier in pack, yes? Remind you when you forget."

I'm trying, Gryka. Maybe when we get it right, when we finally remake ourselves into something that can live in freedom and in beauty without destroying it so we can stay, we'll find you and your pack already there, waiting for us, grinning, measuring our strength. And we'll grin too, exposing big sharp teeth of our own, and we'll measure your strength, and we'll both say simultaneously "So long as you don't hunt on *our* side of the river," both of us pointing opposite directions, and we'll laugh and hug and our packs will run together, just this once, because it's a very special time. And we will find the largest herd of the biggest, fastest, most dangerous animals with the sharpest, most wicked horns, and we won't take a small or weak or lame one like we usually do, we'll take the strongest, healthiest male, and we will all eat and eat and eat, splashing around in the bloody carcass like kids in a wading pool and stuffing ourselves with meat until we can barely walk, and then we will lie down on a rock in the sun, and you'll tell me "Welcome home," and I'll reply "Thanks for waiting for us."

———

This is the song of your blood. You have it now. It's in you. It's always been in you, but now you remember. It's up to you. All of us. Now.

You can find us at
www.gnolls.org

LaVergne, TN USA
29 November 2010
206646LV00001B/66/P